TRIPLE CROSS

Graham J. Burlem

TRIPLE CROSS

British Library Cataloguing in Publication Data

Printed and bound in the UK by
Best Seller Books

Pull up a chair and I'll tell you a tale

CHAPTER 1

A funeral was a hell of a place to meet a client. But she'd insisted and besides my mate Jeff had recommended me.

"It's at the Church of England cemetery in Archway." She gave me the address. "One o'clock Thursday! Jeff says you're the best there is. Is that right?"

"I'm still breathing and paying taxes if that's any reference."

"Thursday then! You'll easily recognise me. I'll be in black and crying." The phone clicked and she was gone.

There was just one woman and no more than six or seven men by the grave, so there was no difficulty in identifying her. She was right on both points. She was in black and she was crying. She held a crumpled tissue and dabbed at her tears, then every so often found a small section of it and blew her nose. She was in her early thirties, tall and slim in a black mid-calf-length coat, black wide-brimmed hat, black stockings. Absolutely nothing like I'd imagined from the phone call. She stood beside the minister at the grave head, close to a small chubby chap, the rest of the men in a semicircle around them. I only knew of a couple, Tom Stafford, a chief inspector from Kensington nick and Bobby Hallet, a petty villain with a record as long as the Edgware Road. I was surprised to see them together knowing they probably wished each other was in the coffin instead of Frank.

The window of a car parked in the small roadway skirting the plot opened and someone pointed a camera and started snapping faces. The wind blew through the trees. Clothes flapped. The pall-bearers eased the coffin down, veneered pine rasped against the hard earth. She turned slowly taking in the scene, looked first at the minister then quizzically from face to face at the men behind her. She turned my way and casually eyed me, then went back to staring at the grave.

"For as much as it hath pleased our Lord of his great mercy to take to himself the soul of our dear brother, Frank Harvey, here departed …"

I shivered, unsure if it was the weather or the place. Funerals always made me queasy. I could have been at Steve's playing snooker or sinking a pint instead of standing here like a bottle of milk on a doorstep. Although it's an enquiry agent's lot to hang about, an occupational hazard you might say, waiting for someone to show up or waiting for someone to leave, somewhere they shouldn't have been in the first place.It started drizzling. The rain dampened the brown scattered leaves and the wreaths either side of the grave. I looked over at Tom Stafford with his bald bullet head and bags under his eyes. Bobby stood a few feet from him in trainers and a fleece. His face small and narrow, pock-marked with acne around the mouth, smiling as the ropes were slipped from the coffin. The minister picked up pace.

"Ashes to ashes, dust to dust. In the sure and certain hope …"

The minister was about at the end of his spiel when a maroon-coloured Merc slid to a halt in front of the Daimler hearse. The driver's window slid down and a man in small granny-styled sunglasses with a round face framed in badly permed mop-like hair peered out. An older man got out of the passenger side and into the back. That window slid down too. The unshaven faces stared, unspeaking. The driver lit a cigarette.

Frank's widow eyed me again. Her face pale from a bit too much foundation, her eyes heavy from a bit too much mascara, but her lipstick was blotted just right. She smiled sweetly. It was a pleasant smile revealing a tiny gap between her front teeth. I wondered what she'd invited me into, what with villains and coppers who hated each other standing together and mourners turning up in flash Mercs and lighting up not twenty feet from the grave. The minister made the sign of the cross and Frank had had his send-off.

The man beside the widow also made a cross, then pecked her on the cheek, the others in their dark suits and black ties stood for a moment slightly embarrassed, waiting their cue from Lisa. I felt awkward in Levis, open-neck shirt and leather jacket, even if the jacket did cost three hundred quid. The minister touched her arm, said something, she smiled, then stared at the open grave where drizzle now fell on the casket and blew it a kiss. Then after several mourners had offered their condolences and kisses, she made her way over to me.

"Mister Sutton, Eddie Sutton? Thanks for coming. You're just like Jeff said you was."

"Sorry to hear about your husband."

"Thank you." She introduced the tubby guy as Clive, her brother. "I'm still numbed; everything's 'appened so quick." Tears welled up and rolled down her already wet cheeks so that rain and tears mixed together and streaked the foundation. She leaned against Clive. "Just over forty," she sobbed. "Can you believe that! Just over forty."

I said I was sorry again and then asked how I could help her.

"You can help all right. First off, by seeing me home. There's not going to be any wake." She nodded in the direction of the cars. "The tall thin one's Bobby Hallet, them in the Merc's George and Terry Norton. They're here for trouble."

"If I'd have known it was a minder's job, I'd …"

"Oh, there's something else as well, don't worry."

"What's that?"

"Help me find a million quid's worth of bent money." She said it quite matter of factly as she popped her tissue into her coat pocket.

"I see, and what do we do if we find it?"

"Why, give it back of course!"

CHAPTER 2

We walked from the graveside to Clive's car parked in the roadway. The drizzle got stronger. Beads of rain meandered down the windscreen. Lisa turned and stared back at the grave where gravediggers hurried to cover Frank. She blew a kiss and whispered she loved him. Then dabbed at fresh tears.We stood about ten feet from the Merc, conscious all the time of four unblinking eyes on us. One of its doors opened and someone got out. He was medium height, thickset with a nose like a mushroom and dark shadows under his eyes. I thought he was going to speak. Instead he just stared. Lisa tightened her grip on Clive.

"It'll be all right, pet!" Clive said. "I was going to take her back," he said to me, "but I think you should. Besides, I know she wants to talk to you."

A scuffle broke out behind us. Bobby had pulled the camera away from its owner, dropped it on the ground and was about to stomp on it when Stafford stepped in front of him.

"That's police property," he said. Bobby smiled. "And very expensive," Stafford added, casually moving his hand and grabbing Bobby by the balls. "That means it cost a lot of money. Understand?"

Bobby's mouth opened, but all he could do was groan. He tried to speak as Stafford slowly twisted his handful, but the words wouldn't come out. He tried again, and again. But all there was, was just a grunting noise. He tried to shift Stafford's hand, but couldn't. His cheeks blew out like he was trying to hang onto his breakfast and then he slowly doubled over.

Stafford smiled. A nasty, spiteful smile.

"So, don't touch what don't belong to you. All right?"

5

Bobby's groan of relief was almost animal sounding as Stafford let go. He lurched forward, then slumped against the car holding his crotch. Stafford walked away. The two in the Merc smiled. Other than that, they hadn't batted an eyelid.

"They couldn't even let me bury my Frank in peace," Lisa exclaimed. "Bastards!"

We drove along a narrow winding road lined with tall willowy trees. A watery sun ahead played peek-a-boo behind outstretched branches. I turned left past the two-storey red brick chapel, where not long before they'd said prayers for Frank Harvey. The beds of pansies either side of the door shafted mauves and yellows into what was otherwise a day as grey as the marble headstones. I turned through the large wrought-iron gates onto the main road past blocks of flats and petrol stations where life went on.

"Where to?" I asked.

"I live in Islington. D'you know it?"

"I know the Emirates."

"How come the Arsenal?"

"I was brought up not far from there. Got taken to the Gunners as a kid by my dad when he was off duty and it sort of stuck."

I gunned the engine and sped through lazy afternoon suburbs with almost deserted pavements towards Islington. Years ago it had been a North London backwater and then in the eighties and nineties pop stars and TV celebs had discovered its handsome houses and beautiful garden squares and the fact that it lay right between the City and the West End. Now it was gentrified, which meant that those that couldn't afford Hampstead had moved in and helped jack up the Islington values.

We'd gone almost two miles with only the hum of the wheels and the drone of the engine between us before she asked if we were being followed. I looked in the driver's mirror, but there was nothing suspicious behind us.

"Who are you expecting?"

"Those bastards in the Merc." I took another look, but there wasn't anything there. "It's a long story. It's the reason I asked you here today. Them," she said, throwing her thumb over her shoulder at imagined pursuers, "them and a geezer called Don Taylor and my Franky did a job. Oh! And Bobby Hallet, he was in on it too. Five of them, right! They turned over a jeweller's in Kensington. It should have been a doddle. But it all went wrong." She fell into momentary silence. Don Taylor rang a distant cord. I was fumbling with my memory when she said, "Like falling of a bleeding log, my Frank said."

"But it wasn't?"

"He got the loot all right, ten million quid's worth. Jewellery, stones, mostly stones in necklaces and pendants, stuff in for repair, stuff in for valuation, maybe not all belonging to the jeweller's but all on the premises. They hit the jackpot. It was a right killing!"

"But?"

"He also got nicked. That's what he was on remand awaiting trial for."

This time the silence between us was longer. I checked my driver's mirror again. And there was the Merc four cars down, not quite tucked in behind a removal lorry. I slowed and took a left.

"You're going the wrong way!"

"Their car's turned up."

She twisted around as it pulled right out from behind the lorry.

"Bastards!" she spat. I horsed around for a few turnings, then came back onto the main road and hit the accelerator. "Can't you lose them?"

"Wait." I sped for a few hundred yards. Their car got closer. Ahead were the traffic lights with Holloway Road. I couldn't make up my mind whether to jump them or handbrake them. I slowed allowing them to close right up, then at the last moment turned a violent left. Lisa slumped against me as the car screeched sideways. The Merc sailed past too late to make the turn. I gunned the engine through some back turnings then came back onto the main road. I checked my mirror I don't know how many times. But they weren't there.

CHAPTER 3

We turned into a wide Islington street with terraces of flat-fronted period houses.

"This is Westbourne Lodge Road," she said. "I live at the bottom. Not far." I was expecting Islington glitzy, but this was the poorer part. "Just over there. Just on your left," she said.

I pulled into a small ex-council estate of three-storey maisonettes, all identical except for the colour of the front doors. It reminded me of my own upbringing on a council estate in Clapton, North East London, through the seventies. A couple of lads opposite on bikes skidded on the roadway beside garages with AFC scrolled across the doors. I parked wondering what they'd nick off the Beema and followed her in.

It was small like a mini-townhouse, with a cloakroom and a bedroom on the ground floor painted in magnolia. She led me upstairs into a large living room and pulled back the curtains allowing late afternoon sunshine to flood the room. There was a green sofa against the far wall, a couple of matching easy chairs and a TV with a plant on it. She took off her hat and shook her hair. It hardly moved because it was cut so short, almost clipped, but in a well-cut way. She ran her hand through it, took off her coat and asked for my jacket.

"Have a seat. I should take the sofa, it's the comfiest."

The furniture was cheap except for the television. There were a couple of paintings, a Lowry and a ship on the high seas, photos of Frank and her on a dresser beside a couple of vases of carnations, a wedding snap on the steps of a church. She, slimmer, in a long white dress holding a posy of lilies, her blond hair shoulder length, her face thinner, heavily powdered, her eyes made up with thick mascara. The groom was tall, slim, with an angular face, square jaw, long black hair over his ears, his thin nose becoming slightly bulbous at the nostrils, but still a handsome man for all that. He wore a dark suit with a white shirt and grey tie. He smiled but looked uncomfortable. There were other snaps of the two of them somewhere in the sun, her in a skirt and shirt, him in jeans and T-shirt holding her around the waist. She asked if I wanted a drink. But I declined.

"You won't mind if I do." She opened the door of a dresser and poured herself a neat one. "Cheers! They call it mother's ruin. Funny how drinks get names. Franky says, I mean he used to say, that is, what I mean is, oh, shit!" she exclaimed, wiping her eyes.

"You all right?"

"Yeah, yeah." She took a nip, then gulped the rest and wiped her eyes again with the back of her hand.

"How long were you married?"

"Seventeen years. I was nineteen, a hairdresser. He was twenty-five. A car mechanic by trade. I knew he'd had his run-ins with the law, but I thought he was the greatest thing since sliced bread." She asked again if I'd have a drink.

"No thanks."

"I thought marriage might change him but …"

"Talking of Frank, you never finished your story."

She rested the glass on the arm of an easy chair and said,

"Ever 'eard of a jeweller's called Weindenfeldt's?"

I knew of them and why I knew Don Taylor's name.

It all came back to me. Because for three days last summer they'd been the headlines on TV and in the newspapers. Five of them in a stolen car had parked up on the pavement outside a jeweller's in High Street Ken, a hundred-odd yards from St Mary Abbots Church at about nine in the morning. It had been a warm sunny July Friday with a Wedgwood-blue sky. There was some traffic. But by and large Kensington hadn't quite woken up yet. They'd waited as members of staff were buzzed in as they arrived. One, two, and then when the door opened for the last one, four of them, by now in masks and tooled up like the Marines, crashed in. One of them pulled the door blinds down while another put a round from a sawn-off into the ceiling, then ordered everyone on the floor face down. Meanwhile Terry sat in the Jag like it was just another day's work.

"I remember it," I said.

She finished her drink and poured herself another.

"My Frank and George held the staff down while Don and Bobby cleared the showcases and the safe of everything, absolutely everything. It's a wonder they didn't nick the loo rolls."

I also remembered the punchline to the robbery. The bit that the media had loved. The four then had strolled out of the shop back to the Jag, no haste, no panic, as casual as you like. Terry revved up and pulled away from the kerb just as a cab completed a U-turn from the opposite side of the road between the long banks of traffic islands that divide the wide carriageways along there. The vehicles collided. The cab's wheel arch got tangled with the Jag's bumper. Terry reversed hard, trying to disengage. Meanwhile the cabby was out of his taxi banging on their window. Terry tried reversing again only ripping the wheel arch further, sending the cab driver nuts. Then Don got out of the motor yelling, screaming, swearing at the taxi driver to back up, then stuck the sawn-off in his face. By now a knot of traffic had developed behind them, one, a few cars down, was an unmarked diplomatic protection security patrol group car on its way back to Palace Gate in Kensington, where all the embassies are. That's how the copper came to have a gun. He got out of his car to investigate what was happening. He saw the shooter, yelled 'armed officer, drop your weapon'. Maybe Don would have. Maybe not. Who knows? But as he turned, weapon still in hand, the officer discharged one round right into Don's heart.

"I remember it," I said, "everything."

"Just a fluke! All of it, just a fluke," she murmured. "A million-to-one chance!"

She was right. But sometimes it's the stuff a life is made of. Or a death. From the start of the robbery to Don hitting the pavement had taken all of eight and a half minutes!

"They reckon Don was probably dead before he hit the ground."

"That's the way they're trained." I said.

She gave me a sideways glance and said,

"Once a copper, always a copper, I suppose! There was mayhem, well, you can imagine, pedestrians screaming, running. Some towards the shop, others away from it. The cops not sure what they were dealing with. Absolute bedlam. And while it's all kicking off Frank gets out the motor and legged it. George almost followed then changed his mind, got back in it, and Terry finally got them away."

"Who had the gear?"

"Frank."

"That was handy!"

The phone rang. She picked up the receiver. A quizzical look spread across her face and then it turned ashen. She listened for a few moments longer, then the receiver more or less fell out of her hand. She lifted her glass and finished the lot.

"What's the matter, Lisa?"

"It's started again. I knew it would. I'm surprised those bastards didn't have a go at the funeral."

"What's started? Who was that?"

"George Norton. Mister headcase himself."

"You mean the one that followed us?"

"Trying to scare me off."

"Off what?"

"What d'you think? Looking for the jewellery."

"What did he say?"

"It doesn't matter, 'cause he's not going to stop me. He's been on my case one way and another, from the start, for nearly three months, wanting to know what Frank might have told me. Did I know where the jewellery was stashed? He tried threats. Then intimidation and finally realised Frank hadn't told me anything so as to keep me safe."

The liquor had put a little colour into her face, but you could tell she'd had a fright. Even so, I could see what Frank saw in her, she was an attractive woman, tall, slim, with a good figure. And I got to thinking what a shame she was so recently widowed. Or who knows?

"I'm not sure what you're on about, Lisa. But you better give this some serious thought. Anyone that can blast his way into a jeweller's isn't going to be too concerned about smacking you around. Or worse." The phone rang again. She looked at it for a long time. "Here, let me."

She shook her head.

"No, I'm ready for him this time." She grabbed up the receiver. The hard lines around her mouth were even deeper. "It's Clive," she said. "Yes, Clive. No problems at all. Yes, he's still here. Yes, love, I'm fine. I'll ring in the morning and thanks again for being with me today. You're a real sweetie." She held her head then closed her eyes. "I thought ..."

"You'd best sit down."

"It was nice of you to have offered to answer the phone. Especially as George knows you're involved."

"Am I?"

"Involved?" She refilled her glass. "Oh, yeah! You are now."

"Really? Well, you've got another think coming. At least until I know what's cooking here!"

"You're in it, whether you like it or not. Even if you quit now he'll keep tabs on you for the next couple of months. He's that sort.

As for what's cooking? It's like I said at the funeral. About a million quid's worth of bent money."

I watched her twiddling her glass as she spoke. She looked at the bottle as though deciding about a third.

"You know the more I hear, the less I like all this."

"What about fifty thousand in your bin, all strictly kosher, like that?"

"Maybe I'll have that drink after all."

"What'll it be? Scotch, brandy?"

"Coffee, please."

I followed her into the kitchen, which was small and square. It looked like a B&Q do-it-yourself job with white wood wall and floor units, and grey worktop surfaces. She put a cup and saucer out, then filled the kettle.

"What happened after the robbery, with the share-out and so forth?" I asked.

"I'm about to take a big chance on you. I just hope you're worth it."

"So do I."

She told me that the five of them were supposed to meet up with the fence for the share-out on the following Sunday morning at George and Terry's car breaker's yard over in Brixton. But that Frank had planned to double-cross them. He'd set up a deal with a different fence for the Saturday night, and turned the jewellery for a million cash. The plan was a fifty–fifty share-out with a mate of his, then off abroad where Lisa would have joined him.

"'Cause George and the others don't know this," she said, waiting for the kettle to boil. "As far as they're concerned, the jewellery's still stashed somewhere."

"So where does the fifty grand come in?"

"You asked me earlier what we …"

"We?"

"I should do if I found the money. Let me ask you the same question."

"You said it before. Once a copper, always a copper! Go to the police."

"Nearly right. Go to the insurers. Frank's brief reckons they would cough up a finder's reward for the fenced money. Not the jewellery, because who knows where the hell that is now. But the payout."

Steam plumed from the kettle clouding the windows. She made coffee and handed it to me.

"Help yourself to sugar."

"No thanks. Trying to watch my weight."

She looked me up and down.

"You don't look as though you've got much to worry about. What are you, forty?"

"Forty-one."

"Most of the blokes I know in their forties have already started a beer gut." I stirred in some milk. She gave me another once-over. "You must work out."

"How much does he reckon this brief of Frank's?"

"Ten per cent. On a million. Do the maths! Fifty grand each."

"Just like that!"

"Yes, as a matter of fact, exactly like that! Well, not exactly like that. The insurers would pay the reward all right. But not to me 'cause I'm Frank's widow and Frank's the one that nicked the stuff in the first place."

I could see the logic. The board being embarrassed if a newspaper or a shareholder got hold of the story.

"That's why it's not worth my while even co-operating with their insurance investigators. But I want the money. Maybe fifty grand's not a lot to you …"

"Lisa, fifty grand's fifty grand! Believe me, I ain't knocking it." And I wouldn't. I liked and appreciated money. I liked what it bought, like my new Beema, good clothes, eating in good restaurants. There's something nice and warm and reassuring about having money, especially if you've been brought up without it, which I was. But I've managed to make good through some luck. But mainly hard work. I liked that reassuring feeling. I liked it a lot. Not that money's my be-all and end-all. It says in the Bible you should give to the poor, which I agree with, but nowhere does it say you should be one of them.

"I won't bore you with an autobiography Eddie. But life hasn't been a bed of roses. Clive and me were orphaned when we was kids and brought up by an aunt who was as mad as a March hare. I loved my Frank. But him doing bird every five minutes and now losing him hasn't made for an easy life. Fifty grand won't bring him back, but it would be a brilliant little nest egg against the future."

"I can see that."

"Look, if the truth be told," she went on, "I could do without all this, dredging up the past. Especially with a stranger. But I want the reward, which means I have to take chances, and one of them's on the help I get."

"What exactly is the help you want?"

"Someone to co-operate with in finding the money and then fronting for both of us in getting the finder's fee with me in the background."

"I see."

"You were recommended. But I've no real way of knowing if you're any good."

"Thanks a lot!"

"On the other hand I'm no match on my own for George, Terry, Bobby or the insurance people. So I'm stuck with taking a risk."

I stirred my coffee and thought about all she'd said.

"Who was the fence?" I asked.

She paused for a long time busying herself unnecessarily, sweeping up a few coffee granules that had fallen on the kitchen worktop. I suppose in the end she decided to take a gamble because she said,

"Ralph Leyton. He owns a jeweller's-cum-pawnshop in Queensway."

"And Frank's partner?"

"I don't know."

"Do me a favour, Lisa!"

"Honest. Frank only told me about the blag the night before and that he'd be holed up in some B&B for two nights until the stuff was fenced. That's how it come out about the double-cross. I asked him when the five was meeting. He smiled and said it was just going to be two of them."

"But you must have asked him who?"

"Course! But he wouldn't say. But it stands to reason it was one of the other four."

I'd only had a few sips of the coffee when the doorbell rang. Two long definite rings letting you know the caller meant business. She went to the window and hesitantly twitched the curtain taking a sideways glance.

"Great! That's all I bloody needed," she cursed.

CHAPTER 4

I stood in the narrow hallway as she opened the front door.

"Yees!" she exclaimed in mock greeting. "And what can I do for you?"

"Hello, Lisa, remember me? Detective Chief Inspector Stafford. This is DC Longton; we're here to offer our condolences. Mind if we come in?" and not waiting for an answer barged past her. "Wipe your feet," Stafford said, without turning around. "Wouldn't want Mrs Harvey to get a bad impression about the police." He stopped a couple of feet from me looking me up and down like I was a box of something he couldn't make up his mind about buying. "Good afternoon. I'm Chief Inspector Stafford and this is ..."

"I heard."

"And you'd be?"

"A friend of Mrs Harvey's."

That nasty little smile I'd seen earlier as he twisted Bobby's balls broke at the corner of his thick lips.

"How cosy! Sorry to hear about Frank, Lisa."

"I can imagine!"

"I was at the funeral."

"It would have been hard to miss you."

"Oh, Hallet, you mean. Got lots of snaps."

Lisa stood beside me. The pair of us blocking the hall and making the point he wasn't going to be invited any further.

"Yes, lots of nice snaps."

"Well, now you've delivered your condolences you can piss off!"

"I heard a little bit of gossip about you the other day, Lisa. That's why I'm here." He turned to Longton, a twenty-something with blond hair wearing a shirt with a collar size too large. "Remember me mentioning it to you, Longton, that Mrs Harvey had come up in conversation?"

"That's right, guv. I remember it clearly."

"Shouldn't you be sitting on his knee with your hand up your shirt when you speak, sonny!" Lisa exclaimed.

Longton, who'd been enjoying Stafford's authority, started to say something but nothing came out.

"Just the other day it was," Stafford added.

"And what did you hear? That I'd cancelled my standing order to police charity?"

"Much worse. Much, much, much worse. That you're looking for the jewellery."

"What jewellery's that?"

"The stuff your husband and his lowlife friends nicked."

Lisa made an exaggerated gesture of pulling back her sleeve and checking her watch.

"Is that the time! Tut, tut, you mustn't let me keep you."

"You get in the way of my investigations, Mrs Harvey, and I'll nick you so fast you'll think you're dreaming." He looked around the hall, then craned his neck to cop a look into the rooms. "You've redecorated since I was last here."

"I wonder if it was anything to do with the state you left the place in. Can you believe it?" she said turning to me. "I'm sitting here that Saturday night watching the telly. They didn't even ring, just zapped the door open. You 'ad to be here to believe it. Him and Christ knows how many others. All stab vests and BO."

"We just wanted a word with Frank."

"But the fact he wasn't here didn't stop you taking the place apart. Did it? Did it?" she spat. "All those questions, Jesus! You wouldn't believe it. Where was he? When did I last see him? What did I know about the blag? On and on, until it was nearly daylight."

"And Lisa only made one mistake. Didn't you? That's why she's got the hump."

"And what was that?" I asked.

"Shall I tell him or will you?" Lisa was silent, her chin on her chest. "Oh, well, if you insist. She'd written down the number of the B&B where Frank was holed up on a pad. The biro left an imprint on the other pages. Longton here found it, phoned the exchange, discovered what it was, put two and two together, and well, there you go! I don't think I've left anything out, have I, Lisa?"

"But how did you know it was Frank you were after in the first place?" I asked.

"From information received."

"You mean Frank was grassed?"

She lifted her head slowly and looked right into Stafford's eyes.

"Such an emotive word that. Wouldn't you say that was an emotive word, Longton?"

"Definitely emotive, guv."

"You bastard!" Lisa said. "You bastard. Grassed! You know I never realised that before. That someone grassed my Frank."

"I think it's time for you to leave, Chief Inspector. You and the DC. Mrs Harvey's had quite a day. She needs to get some rest."

"I'll let you know when I'm ready to go," Stafford replied.

I clicked on my mobile.

"Well, let's see what her brief thinks. Or would you like to try grabbing my bollocks to stop me?"

Stafford squared his shoulders.

"Well, on second thoughts. It must have been quite a rough day popping Frank in a box and all. I dare say you're right." He moved close to Lisa, his head almost touching hers. "Just remember what I said. So fast you'll think you're dreaming. I didn't get your name," he said turning to me.

"I didn't give it."

"No need to show us out. I know the way."

CHAPTER 5

She sat on the sofa, staring into nothing.

"Grassed?"

"Had to be. Job like that. It'd take the police forty-eight hours to get a handle on things. Never mind having a suspect."

"But who, and why?"

"The second bit's easy. Someone annoyed with Frank having the gear. Not a gang member, because you say they were still expecting to meet on the Sunday. But somebody privy to what was going on who you don't know about."

She gave me the sweetest smile. Her lips pulled back lightening up her face. Which I hoped meant she was a little more reassured about my competence.

"Jeff was right. You are good. How much d'you think Stafford knows?"

"Not much. What you saw was a fishing expedition."

"Thanks for getting rid of him." She drew her legs under her and covered her knees with her skirt. "Quite a story, isn't it? It gets worse. Frank met with Leyton the Saturday night and fenced the gear for a million quid."

"Then what?"

"The idea was to take the dough back to the B&B and then off to Northern Cyprus in the early hours of Sunday morning. He knew the captain of a cargo boat in Liverpool who'd take him to Hamburg, then he'd get a budget flight to Kyrenia on a moody passport."

"Why Northern Cyprus?"

"No extradition treaty with the UK. And apparently not too many questions asked about where your money comes from."

"And then you and your kids would have joined him?"

"Just me. I've miscarried twice. The doctors advised against trying again. I suppose the good Lord gives each of us a cross to bear. I suppose it makes sense to him. My faith gives me strength. Franky wasn't one for religion. You wouldn't have expected it in his line of business."

So it was just Lisa and no baggage. Things were looking quite bright. But I had to smile at the phrase 'his line of business', which meant thieving and scaring people shitless!

"But I believe," she added. She touched a little gold cross around her neck. "I believe."

"So it was you and Frank and his share of a million, and a trip to Cyprus. Nice one!"

"Or would have been if he hadn't been nicked."

"So how come the police didn't find the dough?"

"I told you it got worse. Someone tried to attack him on the way back from Ralph's. He fought them off. Got away. But he was certain it wasn't coincidence. So he hid the dough until he was off."

"Then got nicked."

"Yes."

"And now he's dead and the dough's still missing?"

"In spades!"

I looked at Lisa sitting there. Frank's death and the day's events written in lines on her ashen face. But wondered nevertheless if she was legit or trying to take yours truly for a ride. I just couldn't decide for the moment.

"Any idea where it might be?" I asked.

She shrugged.

"Like I say, he wouldn't say so as to keep me safe."

"A safety-deposit box maybe?"

"I doubt there would have been one open that time of night."

"Did he have any bank direct debits?"

She smiled, then broke into a laugh. Her face momentarily lit up again erasing the day's aggro.

"You serious! His line of work was taking money out of banks. Not putting it in."

"I suppose so."

"Why d'you ask?"

"I thought he might still be paying out on the rental of one." I wondered where you'd hide that kind of money. "Maybe he sent it to Cyprus?"

"How? He didn't know where he'd be till he got there."

"That only leaves the B&B." She nodded. "But the police must have searched it."

"Inch by inch. As did George, Terry and Bobby."

"So you think I'll be able to do what the Met and three seasoned villains couldn't?" She nodded. "I'm touched by your confidence. But I don't think we'll find anything. Then again …"

"Fifty grand's fifty grand. Does that mean you'll give it a go?"

"Why not!"

"Just one thing we get clear now. If you don't find nothing there's nothing to come from me."

"Agreed. I've got a condition too. If after a couple of weeks I'm not getting anywhere, I'm at liberty to just walk off the job."

"Agreed." We shook hands; she had a decent grip. She suggested we put the whole thing in writing. "Is there anything else you need?"

"A photo of Frank, please."

She opened her handbag and slipped a photo of him from her wallet. It was a head and shoulders job. The man in the wedding snap had put on a few years. He was still handsome with those lean features and square jaw and had a warm smile that added to the looks. But there were lines around the eyes now and his hair was flecked with grey.

"It was taken last summer, just before the blag," she said staring at it. "He was a good-looking bloke, my Frank, don't you think?"

"What happened?"

"You mean …? He was in the prison dining hall taking his food to a table. He just keeled over. At first the screws thought he was up to something; when they realised it was legit they got a doctor who put him in the 'ospital. At first he seemed to be getting better. Then a few days after the attack he had another, and that was that." She held her face in her hands. I thought she was going to cry but she didn't. "Anything else?" she asked after a few moments.

"His personal effects."

She bit her lip and pointed at the dresser from where she'd taken the gin. They were in a large manila envelope: a few paperbacks, a comb, a brush, a gold ring, some ballpoint pens and a toothbrush.

"Not much to show for a man's life, is it."

"Others have less."

"And others more. A lot more."

"He left you all this," I said, sweeping an arm over the room. "And a million pounds. Some people leave nothing to note that they passed this way. Not even a toothbrush."

"I suppose. It's just that I had such high expectations for us."

I laid it all out on the dresser top. She picked up the gold ring.

"This was his wedding ring," she said holding it lovingly. "You see here I had it engraved, from L to F with love. You should have seen his face when I give it him. He said he'd never take off 'is finger. People didn't understand my Frank."

"You'll be telling me next, he was thinking about getting a job with the Samaritans."

"He did what he thought he had to. That's how he was brought up. He wanted to provide for me. That's how he managed it. Doing what he did. Maybe you would too if you was brought up in a council flat with your dad working light till dark on the railways and your mum too busy for you 'cause she took in washing to make ends meet?"

"Any of this other stuff mean anything to you?"

"Not really." She fingered the books which were all Wilbur Smith except for one on crosswords.

"And the prison didn't send you anything else?"

"Only his jacket and trousers." She went to the bedroom and got them for me. A blue wool jacket that had seen better days and grey M&S trousers.

"It's strange," I said. "I can't believe someone like Frank wouldn't have tried to let you know where he'd hidden the money, on the basis he might not survive."

"You're right!"

"When did he last phone?"

"A few days before …"

"Did he ever write?"

"He wrote me while he was in the 'ospital, a real screwy letter. I thought he must have done it while he was under the doctors with all them drugs they give him."

She went to the bedroom again and came back with the letter. It was a sheet of thin white flimsy prison paper. The writing was in ballpoint in an almost childlike hand.

Hiya Babe,

I hope you're all right and everything's okay. The old ticker's behaving now and I'm hoping to get back to normal soon. Being in the hospital gives you time to think. You know what popped into my head the other night, don't laugh. Our holiday last year, that B&B we stopped at in Benidorm. All that aggro with the rooms. Remember we finally got settled in room 12. You're sitting there having your vodka and orange and I'm trying to finish a crossword. Trying to get the last two clues. It's always the last two that are the most important, the ones you need to concentrate on. What was it? A wind that's spent and when is a dish that's a dish not a dish? And then the manager comes up and says there's been a mistake and we've got to move again. And as he's left you've thrown your vodka and orange right at the door. I mean right at. It's funny what comes into your head, ain't it? I'm beginning to feel a bit tired now but I'm okay in myself. But I'm gonna close. So lots of love. See you soon, babe.

And underneath just signed Frank, and three xs.

"What d'you make of it?" I asked, handing it back.

"He must have been drugged to the eyeballs when he wrote this 'cause we've never been to Benidorm. And if I drink, it's only white wine or gin. I wouldn't touch vodka 'cause it brings me out in a rash and he knows it."

"So?"

"Well, you don't need to be a rocket scientist to know what this is."

"You don't?"

"It's Frank trying to tell me where the money is, like you said. You just need to be a bloody rocket scientist to understand it."

"What about the crossword thing?"

She shrugged.

"He was always doing them. Always. He had a knack for them. He could kinda think sideways. But don't ask me what that's got to do with anything."

"What about Benidorm? Sure you've never been there?"

She pulled a face. Then sat on the arm of the sofa and reread the letter.

"Benidorm? Benidorm? What's Benidorm got to do with anything? And vodka and orange? He only ever drank Guinness or Scotch." She looked at the letter and sighed a deep sigh. "Oh, Franky, what are you trying to tell me?"

I put Frank's photo in my wallet and scribbled down my home number next to the printed office and mobile numbers on my card and handed it to her.

26

"Where will you start?"

"At the jeweller's."

"Be lucky! Keep in touch."

I passed a hall mirror just by the front door and caught my reflection. I suppose I wasn't in that bad a nick for forty-one – slim, six foot, black cropped hair, no beer gut, cleft chin – not bad looking, 'quite handsome when you smile' Rita's fond of saying. I suppose it could have been worse. The kids on the bikes were still skidding around on the grey concrete road. I started my car and headed for the gate. As I did, one of them came abreast of the Beema and gobbed right at the window.

CHAPTER 6

Steve's snooker club in Kilburn High Road is where I hang out a
lot. It's a good place for picking up gossip and getting the
whereabouts of faces that need tracing. I walked down the avenue
of tables to the refreshment bar from behind which Steve, an
ex-copper friend of mine, who'd been my DI at Mile Lane in East
London, runs his little gold mine. I sat on a stool and waited as he
finished serving two guys in jeans with shaved heads. The smell of
alcohol and sweat hung in the air. Every so often an explosion of
laughter or swearing rose above the constant hum of voices, balls
cracking, the rasp of cues against tables.

"How you doing?"

"Not bad and you?" He pulled a half pint, wiped the counter and
plonked it in front of me.

"How's crime these days?"

"Not bad."

"Want a game?"

"No time. I'm working."

"Anything tasty?"

"Ever heard of a face named Ralph Leyton?" I asked.

"Leyton, Leyton? Ran a jeweller's in Holland Park,
Queensway, somewhere around there. That was for the legit gear.
But he was well into other stuff."

"Ever nick him?"

"No. A couple of near misses though."

"What was he like?"

"Well, let's see, I've been out of it now, what four years, so
he'd be late fifties, maybe sixty. He's tall, very dapper, very sharp
and crooked enough to hide behind a spiral staircase." He wiped up

some spilt beer. "Four years, Eddie, can you believe it! Four years!"

"Well, I've been out of it for five. So I suppose it must be."

I took a long swig of the beer enjoying the taste and the thirst it quenched.

"D'you miss it?"

"Not any more. I did at first. Not easy making a new life. Don't forget I'd been in it for twenty years. DI for three of them. It was hard at first." He stretched his hand out embracing the snooker hall. "Those bastards that broke my hands that night didn't know what a favour they were doing me. Ending up with all of this." He looked at his hands that were long and thin with knuckles that sat a little too high to the surface and a couple of fingers even now still not quite straight.

"What about you?"

It was a question I asked myself often. What if I was still in the force? Maybe I'd have made DI by now. Maybe. But I wouldn't have the money I have. Or my flat-cum-office. A smart three-bed conversion in Camden Town just on the edge of the West End. One end of the road leading to ever so sedate Regent's Park. The other end to Parkway, with its shops and restaurants. Where for the price of a pint or a cappuccino, you can sit, take the weight off your feet and watch some really serious talent strolling. I've worked hard for what I've got. I put in the hours. I'm not afraid of hard work. It was an ethic I picked up from a hard-working working-class background. But nevertheless. I still miss the camaraderie. The Met's like a family. I have no mother or father. Only a younger married brother. I would like to have been part of a large family. That's maybe why I joined the force in the first place. That's why maybe Steve and I got on so well from day one. Because I saw him as family in some way. Whatever it was, or is, I know I can trust him. He can trust me. He's balding now, poor sod. The dome of his head has hardly any hair on it. But it gets thicker as it gets to the sides and the back of his head. Grey flecked with black. Back then he was clean shaven. Nowadays he has a beard which matches the hair colouring. He has dark small eyes that don't miss a thing set in a round face that smiles most of the time.

"Anyway, it was different for me," I said at last. "I never had an option."

"You was a good DC, Eddie. I still think they could have treated you better. You should have appealed."

"Do me a favour! Anyway, it's all piss down the lav now, isn't it."

"There wasn't a copper in the nick that didn't want to give Farmer a right-hander or two."

"But it was me that did it."

"Piece of shit like that had it coming. So why you interested in Leyton?"

"Remember Frank Harvey and the Weindenfeldt blag?" Steve nodded. "Leyton fenced it."

"Tut, tut, tut, naughty Ralph!" he replied and went off to serve a customer with tea and a meat pie. He came back, poured himself a half, took a sip and put it on a shelf behind him.

"What d'you know about Frank Harvey?"

"Now, he was a very naughty boy. You name it, he'd done it. Started in his early teens robbing milk floats in the days when milkmen carried money. Then graduated to post offices, then building societies. Bit of GBH. Bit of handling. He was married to some …"

"I know. She's hired me. What d'you think about him using Ralph?"

"Why not. He'd have to take it somewhere. Not exactly the sort of stuff you can take to a car boot."

I finished my beer and told him I'd see him later.

"Take it easy!" he replied. "Oh, Eddie, Rita phoned. Said for me to tell you to check your messages occasionally."

30

CHAPTER 7

I stood outside Weindenfeldt's and window-shopped. The sun beat down on the glass. Behind me was the drone of ceaseless traffic. The pavements were full of shoppers and secretaries taking a lunchtime stroll or doing a quick bit of shopping.

8.45 a.m. on a Friday was a good time for a raid. The very first thing in the morning when they were least expecting it. The unlikelihood of there being any customers. The safe would be open for re-stocking the windows, and four blokes against three married women and a middle-aged man would have the place at their mercy. Which is exactly what had happened. Even without an eyeglass you could tell the stuff in the window was expensive. A large diamond ring on the finger of a tanned ornamental hand sparkled against the backdrop of black velvet. The sun caught a clutch of white-gold bracelets spilling out of a display jewel box and spat and flashed colour across the window.

The shop was all thick red carpet and long narrow glass showcases which ran half the length of the room. The ceiling was high and from it hung three crystal chandeliers. Piped music came up from somewhere with a familiar tune you couldn't place, but helped you relax as you spent your dough. A lad of twenty or so in a well-cut suit smiled and asked if he could help. I returned the smile and asked for the manager. And then in the time it takes to straighten your tiara there was a tall man, slightly stooped, in his early sixties, standing where the boy had been. He wore a navy suit, blue shirt and maroon tie. There were wrinkles on his forehead that stretched back into his heavily receding grey hairline. He asked, in a nicely cultured Kensington accent, how he might help.

"Thanks for sparing me the time. I hope my secretary ..."

"Your secretary?" he said. "Secretary? What's this about?"

"You are Mr er, er …"

"Mr Owen."

"Owen, that's right. I'm Renton from the Criminal Inquiries Compensation Authority. We have an appointment for 2 p.m." I produced a calling card, one of an assorted do-it-yourself dozen I carried.

"There must be some mistake. What's this all about?" Owen asked.

"The robbery on the morning of July 20 2012."

His smile faded, his pinky-white face shadowed with a greyish hue.

"It's not something I care to talk about."

"You're going to have to."

"Who did you say you were?" he asked and reread my card.

"I just want some background and circumstances, that's all. It's for a claim by the owner of the car that was stolen for the getaway, who says he was attacked during its theft."

"I told the police everything. Can't you get it from them?"

"Much better from the horse's mouth."

Owen sighed heavily.

"They just crashed in. Almost at their leisure." He twisted a gold wedding ring around and around and around. He caught himself doing it and stopped. Then in a few seconds started again. "There's not a lot to tell. It was a Friday morning, just before nine." His face became greyer and more pained as he dredged up the memories. "Two of the three assistants were already here. They retired after … Anyway, the door buzzer went. I could see it was Mrs Hargreaves, so I opened up. As I did these four yobs crashed in, sending the pair of us sprawling. Then there was a bang. I remember being showered with powdery stuff, ceiling plaster I later learned. After that, everything's still a bit of a blur."

He stopped twisting the ring and began shaking. I imagined him standing there as the gang burst in. It's a wonder he hadn't shit himself. Who knows! Perhaps he had.

"I wanted to resign afterwards, I felt so ghastly. But Mr Weindenfeldt wouldn't hear of it."

"What happened after they were in?"

"Someone ordered us to lie face down on the floor because that's where I remember being most of the time."

"Then what?"

"Two of the men went into the strongroom to the safe. It was open, you see, to re-dress the windows."

"And the other two?"

"Handcuffed myself and the ladies together."

"Didn't anyone see anything from the street?"

"One of them had pulled the window and door blinds down."

"Did they beat you or the ladies up?"

"No. But the two guarding us did a lot of shouting to keep face down. Then at the two in the strongroom. It frightened the life out of us I can tell you."

I noticed the security man standing just inside the front door and asked why he hadn't tried to do something and was told that he'd been hired subsequently.

The shop door opened and a man in a pinstripe suit with a brunette in a green cashmere coat too young to be his daughter came in. Owen turned to the twenty-year-old and indicated he should serve them then turned back to me.

"Well, I hope I've been of some help to you."

"You certainly have. Did you see their faces?"

"No. They wore masks, you know, balaclava-type things with only the eyes showing."

"What about the alarm? Why didn't you press it?"

"It wasn't possible. It's over there by the …" He started to point then dropped his hand. "The alarm was out of reach from where I was on the floor."

"I understand."

"Even if I had been nearer I don't know that I would have pressed it, four of them, two with shotguns," he said slowly, wearily, "against a middle-aged man." He shook his head. "No, I wouldn't have pressed it."

"If it's any consolation, I think you'd have been crazy to. Look what happened afterwards."

"The shooting, you mean?"

"Did you see any of it?"

He shook his head.

"We heard it while we were still on the floor. A lot of garbled shouting, then a bang like a firecracker going off. I think we were more concerned with ourselves than what might be going on out there."

The shop door opened again and a couple in their late twenties came in. From the corner of my eye, I saw a petite blonde have a few words with them, then she came over to Owen and told him it was the engaged couple wanting the solitaire.

"And now I must go," he said to me.

"One last question. Did you see what the jewellery was carried away in?"

"Yes, as a matter of fact. It was a very large green canvas holdall."

We shook hands and I thanked him for his help and left him to his rich customers, his memories, and his ring twisting.

CHAPTER 8

I came down the steps of my flat and pressed the remote to unlock the Beema. I didn't see either of them until they were there in front of me as though appearing from thin air. George Norton, thickset, about five foot six with that mushroom nose and dark eyes, a bull of a man with black greasy hair slicked back. He wore a blue check half-unbuttoned shirt revealing blue lines of a chest tattoo. He looked as though he'd boxed some time in his life. He stood evenly balanced, arms folded, smiling like a man relishing the prospect of a bit of aggro.

"Want a word with you, mate!" he exclaimed.

Brother Terry stood behind me. He wore a leather bomber jacket and faded jeans, thumbs in the waistband like a yob from an early Marlon Brando film. Lisa was right. I'd only been on the case two days and he'd already found out who I was and where I lived.

"Nice stroke you pulled the other day in the car. Some bastard nearly rammed me when I braked."George said,

"You talking to me?"

"No, the fucking lamppost next to you."

Terry dug me in the back with his finger.

"You sound like a right little smart arse," he said. He was taller than George and thinner and about ten years his junior. He had permed hair, a button nose and blue eyes. A bit of a baby face really, but there was a two-inch scar on his upper lip that told you baby had been up to mischief. I folded my fist around the key ring in case George or Terry decided to up the ante. When it came to a street fight I was as good as any and better than most. I'd do Terry first, elbow in the face. Then a key in George's eye. Then finish

Terry with a kick in the balls. See if he felt like Marlon Brando then.

A couple of passers-by, a tall white girl dragging a mixed-race kid and a pensioner, looked our way, but weren't going to get involved, not with these two.

"You're looking for the jewellery, ain't you? Lisa's hired you to find it, ain't she?"George said,

"Lisa, Lisa who?" Terry dug me in the back again. "Tell your brother," I said to George, "if he digs me again I'll break his fingers."

"Oh, yeah!" Terry said with a snigger.

"Yeah!"

"You what!"

"Leave it out, Tel!" George shouted, "you'll get your chance." He took a step closer so he was right in my face. "You tell Lisa Harvey now Frank's out of it, so is she. Understand? Understand?" he shouted.

I felt any second he'd throw a punch. I tightened my grip on the key ring waiting for even the hint of him moving his hand.

"As for you. You can go back to serving summonses or whatever you do."

Terry checked that George had finished speaking. When he was sure he had, he said,

"You know, I don't like you." But he said it without digging me.

"Don't put your nose where it don't belong," George said interrupting Terry, "or I'll cut it off." And then to Terry, "Let's go." The pair walked across the road and took off in the Merc with a U-turn that filled the road with a screech of tyres.

CHAPTER 9

The Parkland Hotel was in Finsbury Park. It was two four-storey grey brick houses linked together in a terrace of derelict properties that looked as though they should have been pulled down to make way for a slum. It was called a hotel, but in reality it was just a bed and breakfast flophouse, mostly for homeless families financed by the DWP or for transients. An ideal place for Frank to hold up in. Dough up front, no questions asked, especially if you were already known. The trees that lined the street were mostly bare now, their branches like spindly arthritic fingers swayed in the wind. I wondered what approach to use to get information and sight of Frank's room. The private investigator, the TV documentary gag or just plain bribery.

The reception area was small with brown threadbare carpeting and peeling wallpaper. The proprietor was also small; he had olive skin, a Zapata moustache and a toupee. I produced another do-it-yourself card, this time from BBC Programme Research and told him I was doing a series on recent big crimes.

"So what can I do for you?" he asked.

"Well, Mr er, er …?"

"Kamoulous."

"Well, Mr Kamoulous. This is the hotel where Frank Harvey of the Kensington jewel raid was arrested, isn't it?"

"How much they paying, the TV, I mean?"

"It's left very much in my hands as chief researcher."

He smiled with a mouth full of horsey teeth.

"Would you like a seat?" He pointed to a large wicker armchair against a wall.

"The money depends …"

"Depends on what?"

"What sort of story you've got to tell and how much you saw."

"I saw everything."

"Okay, let's say five hundred pounds. Seven if we use it."

His phone system, a big plastic box with seven or eight pegs that looked as though you'd have to take it to Sotheby's to have it repaired, and sat on the counter of a small alcove fronting the hall, rang. He picked up the receiver, flipped a peg, said yes, he had rooms vacant, then was back with me.

"It was July; Harvey, only he called himself Houseman, comes into here, says he want to book a room for two nights, I say okay and make the booking. He pays me there and then."

"How much?"

"Forty quids a night."

It sounded cheap. But then the Hilton it wasn't.

"Did he go out at all after he checked in?"

"Once, Saturday about 6 p.m. I don't know what time he come back. Then about 1a.m. Sunday morning there's a ring at the door. At first I thought it was someone locked out. You see, I live on the premises. When I open up, in comes the coppers. They ask me if I had a Frank Harvey staying here. Of course, I say no. Then they show me a picture of Houseman, I mean Harvey, and I tell them the room number. One of them coppers takes me into the office to look at the register." The phone rang again. Kamoulous said yes. Gave the caller some directions and was back with me. "Where was I?"

"The law's looking at the register."

"Yeah, that's right. Listen, you sure this is only worth five hundred quids?"

"There may be more." He smiled. I thought he would. "Depends. I'm waiting on your every word."

"Well, let's see." He thought for a moment, sucked his teeth, then said, "The copper with me tells me to wake Harvey with some story about a fire. So ups I goes. Harvey opens the door and the cops crash in. Ten minutes later they bring him down handcuffed

38

and drive off. Then a load of coppers start questioning me while another load upstairs are tearing the room to pieces. The furniture, the curtains, the walls, the floorboards, the ceiling, everything. I got compensated but it doesn't do your reputation no good, I can tell you. Still, two months' time it'll all be water over the bridges."

"Why's that?"

"I sold this place to developers. They gonna put up a pukka dosshouse here."

"Two months?" He nodded. "What happened after that?"

"I had your blokes down here."

"My blokes?"

"The BBC. Their reporter, that Tina Johnson, she's a big girl. She looks small when you see her on TV but she's tall. And big," he added, cupping his hands on his chest.

"You were saying."

"Well, they sniffed around a while. Then that Sunday afternoon there was a train crash and they all gone to it."

"But the police came back?"

"For a solid week. They checked every room. The yard at the back, even the roof, but they didn't find nothing."

The fluorescent light picked out beads of sweat on Kamoulous's broad forehead beneath the perfectly even layers of his toupee.

"I'm grateful to you. You've been a great help. I wish everyone I interviewed had as good a recall."

"Well, it's not so hard. I just explained it again like I did before when it happened, to the man that's up there at the moment in room twelve. That was Harvey's room. So it's easy to remember it now."

"You mean there's someone up there now?"

"Yeah!"

"Where's the room, Mr Kamoulous?"

"Look, I don't think …"

"Where?"

"Wait until he comes down."

"A key or no money."

He stroked his chin, then took a key from behind him.

"Which floor?"

"First. Straight down the hall on your left."

"Stay here, and don't phone the room, or you can kiss your dough goodbye."

"Phone the room! What d'you think this is, The Dorchester!"

CHAPTER 10

I opened the door of room twelve. A man turned from peering in a wardrobe and in a Scottish accent told me that the room was occupied and to push off. He was tall and blond and there was the faintest whiff of aftershave on him, nice smelling in an expensive way.

"I said the room's occupied."

"I heard you. If you're looking for the jewellery, don't bother. Just about everyone's had a crack at it."

He came across the room and grabbed me by the shirt. I gave him a shove and he staggered back a few steps. I thought he'd make another move on me. Instead, offered a false, nervous, little smile, revealing small white crocodile-like teeth.

"You a copper?" he asked.

The room was what you'd expect for forty quid a night. Eleven foot by nine, magnolia-painted walls and brown carpet the same as downstairs but not threadbare. There was a single bed in the corner, a cheap wooden bedside table and a wardrobe and wash-hand basin by the window. There was a thin heating pipe that ran across the far wall like a scar and from behind it came the sound of rap from the next room. Everything, including the cream plastic light shade, anonymous and serviceable.

"I said are you a copper?"

"No."

"So what's your business?"

"What's yours?" I asked. He handed me a card that read 'Allied Indemnity Insurance, Brian Saxone, Claims Investigator'. "Well, Mister Saxone. Let's hope your investigating's better than your manners."

41

He straightened his well-tailored jacket then combed his hair in the mirror above the wash-hand basin, while his cold grey eyes, set in a long angular face, with beak nose and high forehead, stayed on me.

"So?"

"My name's Eddie Sutton. I'm just making a few inquiries."

"How much do you know about the robbery?"

"Enough."

"Then you'll know if the jewellery's recovered it's my company's property seeing as we've coughed up ten million quid in insurance," which meant he didn't know about it being fenced.

"And if you don't find it, your company'll pay a finder's fee to someone who can. Right?"

"And that would be you, would it?"

"Perhaps."

I took another look around the room at the starkness of it all. At wooden shelves with several cracked tumblers on them. At a fading creased typed notice drawing-pinned to the door regarding action in the event of a fire. It was what it was: a hole-up for transients. I remembered Frank Harvey's letter written just before dying about a hotel room number twelve in Benidorm. This room, of course. It was just a damn shame I couldn't twig the rest of what he was trying to say.

"What makes you think you can find anything, Mister Sutton?"

"I used to be in the I spy club."

"Ha, ha!"

"I knew Frank," I lied. "I know how his mind worked. And maybe his wife knows more than she's telling, and if she does, she's sure as hell not going to tell you because the insurers won't recognise her as a finder."

"We get a lot of people like you, Mister Sutton, wanting to take a percentage of a find."

"How many of them know the thieves that nicked the stuff?"

He adjusted his perfectly positioned tie knot in the mirror, then preened himself some more. He licked a finger and ran it across his eyebrows.

"Okay, maybe we could co-operate."

"Which translates as?"

"Suppose my company retain you to pass on information from Lisa Harvey?"

"No. I don't do business that way."

"Ten per cent if you find it first. Five if I find it thanks to your help?"

"Fifteen and ten."

"That's a lot of money."

"It was a lot of jewellery. Besides, I've access to Lisa." He thought it over and reluctantly agreed. "In writing!"

"If you insist."

"Believe me, I do."

I thought about the finder's fee including proceeds deriving from the jewellery being fenced. But decided to throw that in as a supposed afterthought later on. He told me he'd get something drafted, then asked where he could get hold of me. I gave him my card and scribbled the number of Steve's snooker hall on the back as well. I glanced around the room again, wondering where you could hide a million quid. Under the floorboards? In the ceiling space? But the cops had already looked there. You could buy a lot of cars, and clothes, and holidays with that kind of dough. Instinct, a copper's instinct, told me the money was still here. Somewhere.

"If you need me," Saxone was saying, "try my mobile first."

"What d'you know about Kamoulous?" I asked.

"Nothing."

"I told him I work for the BBC if he should ask you."

Saxone smiled.

We went downstairs. Kamoulous was in the hallway.

"Everything all right?" he asked.

"Fine. I'll be back on Wednesday."

"What about my money?"

"Wednesday!"

I said goodbye to Saxone on the pavement and he took off in a navy Honda Prelude. I looked around for the Nortons in their big, sleek, maroon Merc but the street was empty. I waited until Saxone was out of sight then dialled Allied Indemnity on my mobile. A cute girl's voice answered and put me through to extension 231. I found myself speaking to another girl, who said she was Saxone's assistant. I asked to speak to him but she said he was out. I told her Saxone was an old colleague of mine and as I was passing through London thought we'd get together for a drink.

"His blond hair turning grey yet?". She said it wasn't. "I'm surprised with all the hard work he does. Still the Scots are renowned for being hard workers, aren't they?" She said they were and asked if there was any message. I said no. I'd ring back. Then I dialled Rita to say hello and arrange meeting her. But she was on voicemail.

CHAPTER 11

I pulled into the traffic and headed for Stoke Newington to Lou Jackson's betting shop. I tried Rita again. This time she was engaged. The traffic slowed. At the kerb a female traffic warden wrote a ticket and the Beatles song 'Lovely Rita Meter Maid' popped into my head, making me smile. Not that that's the song I associate with my Rita. That's the Stones 'Let's Spend the Night Together' because that's what seemed to be playing a lot over the voices and the noise that night in that small Maida Vale flat where we met, and now it always reminds me of her. I hummed a few bars, sang some words as far as I could remember them and smiled again.

"Just having a few friends round, *bach*," Bryn had said, but the living room was so crowded you could hardly move. The windows were clouded with condensation. The air felt as though it had already been in a half-dozen other pairs of lungs. Then the slap on the back, a copper's grip on the shoulder, light yet firm.

"How goes it, *boyo*?"

"Nice party, Bryn."

"Every flat should have a warming."

Someone pushed into him from behind. We turned around; a tall brunette looking a little matronly in a black dress and long necklace swayed glass in hand. Bryn put an arm around her waist and drew her to him.

"Rita, my love, meet a mate of mine, Eddie Sutton. Eddie, this is Rita."

I say hello. She says hello to me, hiccups then giggles. The giggles split her flushed face into a beautiful warm smile.

"Bryn, you must introduce me to your friend," she says.

45

"I already did."

She takes his chin between her finger and thumb and says so you did and hiccups again, says sorry and covers her mouth with her hand. It's then I notice the wedding and engagement rings, a heart-shaped diamond and a plain white-gold band. Bryn says he has to go. We're left together facing each other. She smiles and asks if I'm drinking. I eye the cleavage and wonder if anyone is going to claim her. I tell her I've been known to let a glass of wine pass my lips. She twiddles her empty glass in front of me and says,

" So have I."

We pushed our way into the kitchen and I poured us each a glass. Mick Jagger suddenly filled the flat with 'Let's Spend the Night Together'.

"Where d'you know Bryn from?" she asked.

"I used to work with him."

"Not another copper?"

"Used to be. I'm an enquiry agent now."

"Yes, come to think of it, you look the type."

"What's the type?"

She ran a finger around the rim of her glass then slowly licked it and my blood somersaulted in my veins.

"D'you carry a gun?"

"Only in Maida Vale."

She started to say something and the penny dropped.

"Ha, ha!"

I told her the work's mundane. She didn't believe me so I spin her a few yarns about bank robbers and London lowlifes.

"Are you here on your own?"

"Yes. And you?"

"Yes. Normally I'd be with Henry, my husband, but he's away, up north. He's in ladies' shoes."

"Let's hope the police don't stop him."

She laughed a deep throaty laugh. I asked her where she knew Bryn from.

"We used to be neighbours until boring Henry started making money and decided we should move to Crouch End. And now we're almost neighbours again."

"Crouch End, Maida Vale?"

"It's not that far."

"Not if you're Lewis Hamilton it's not."

Full red lips parted in another smile. Lips that told you, you'd never forget a kiss from her.

Some people crowded into the kitchen so she stood closer to me. Someone reached for a bottle and accidently knocked my drink.

"Sorry, mate!"

"It's okay." I took a handkerchief out and wiped the side of my mouth. Was about to put it back when she took it from me and said,

"Here, you missed a bit!"

"Whatever would I do without you?"

"My good deed for the day."

"10 p.m. You left it late."

"Well, some things are worth waiting for, aren't they?" She put the handkerchief back in my hand and hers stayed there a second longer than was necessary.

We chatted for nearly an hour, half my mind's on the conversation, the other half wondering what she's like in bed. She liked books, films, eating out but not Chinese.

"I can't stand rice. It makes me so fat."

The party began breaking up. Suddenly you could hear yourself speak. There was air to breathe. She wondered where Bryn was so she could say goodbye. I offered her a lift but she declined. We shook hands. I offered her a lift again. But she declined a second time. I watched her walking away, eyeing the legs.

I phoned Bryn the next day for her telephone number. We exchanged pleasantries, chatted about the party, then I asked her out. She resisted, but I persisted.

"I know a nice little restaurant, not a spec of rice anywhere."

She laughed, hesitated, then said yes. We went to a small French bistro I know in Hampstead, then back to my flat for a couple of drinks and ended up in bed.

That had been September a year ago. The evenings were still warm. You could sit in the garden of a pub or drive down to the coast. The seasons had changed, so had she. Maybe someone she cared about and good sex were having a positive effect, because she no longer wore mid-calf skirts. Now it was well-above-the-knee stuff or tight jeans. Her nails were always beautifully manicured. She no longer wore her hair high and swept to one side, but long and centre-parted and loose to her shoulders. And she'd sometimes like to tease me turning up in something tight and no bra.

We saw each other regularly as far as work permitted. She'd even stay at my place overnight, but that was when Henry was out of town, although once or twice she'd come up with a good excuse to be absent without leave. I wondered what he made of it all. If he'd tumbled, he wasn't saying anything.

CHAPTER 12

Lou Jackson's betting shop was crowded. The punters stood in ones and twos looking at the screens or sat at the small tables studying form in the papers. A couple picked their noses as they tried to pick winners. The largest of the televisions broadcast the 2.15 p.m. from Chepstow. The voice of the commentator with his flat diction rose above the voices, the clatter, and the tills every so often ringing up.

I stood by the far wall lined with the day's racing pages, watching a bank of TV screens conveying the latest odds and their movement at various meetings. I looked down the runners and riders for the 2.30p.m. at Haydock. There was a horse called Rita's Man, a second favourite at 4–1. I decided to have a tenner to win. Nearby Bobby Hallet, in jeans and a leather jacket with sleeves hitched to the elbows, straightened up several of the racing papers that had slipped out of their wall frames.

"Got a tip for us, Bobby?"

"Well, if ain't Sherlock Holmes."

A few faces turned from the banks of TVs and clocked us. Bobby smiled, but with no humour in his face. The bright fluorescent lights caught the acne around his mouth making the red vesicles beneath a two-day growth look harsh and sore and the face, rodent-like with its thin lips and pointed nose, even uglier than he already was.

"This, your chosen profession now?"

"It's just a fill-in between jobs as a brain surgeon."

I grabbed him by his jacket and pulled him towards me.

"I didn't think people with form could work in betting offices. The manager know you done bird?"

"He won't care."

"I'll put a word in his ear, shall I?"

"All right, all right, what d'you want?"

"You still up to strokes?"

He straightened his jacket and the shirt underneath it.

"I've given all that up."

"After your little effort in High Street Ken?"

"Dunno what you mean!"

"Dunno what you mean!" I mocked. "Lisa Harvey's marked my card."

His pupils moved nervously, on me then everywhere else but me. Then back on me again. He searched my face to see if I was bluffing about telling his boss and decided I wasn't, because he said,

"That was part of it. It was my missus also, she ..."

"Lend us a hanky, Bobby, I think I'm going to cry."

"Honest, I do a few hours here a week cleaning up, doing the papers, sometimes on the till and a few hours helping my brother-in-law painting and decorating."

"Painting and decorating! Do me a favour! You wouldn't know how to open a can of paint without gelignite."

A voice on the large screen announced they were off at Thirsk, its hollow sound reaching every part of the shop as nine nags took off in a bolt round the course in glorious Technicolor. He tried to walk away but I pulled him back.

"Why d'you go to Frank's funeral?"

"Personal reasons."

"Think someone hid the jewellery in his coffin?"

"Very funny! What d'you want with me, anyway?"

"Information."

"Ring 118."

"It's worth a monkey."

"What makes you think I'd take money off you?"

"'Cause you're a greedy little shit-pot."

"I still remember what you did to my mate Joey. You haven't forgotten Joey Farmer, have you?" He held my stare. "He still has trouble from that nose you give him."

Joey's speciality was getting au pairs hooked on dope then putting them on the game. One had died of septicaemia; that's why I was interviewing him. We were in a small CID interview room in Mile Lane nick, night-time. Joey sits legs outstretched. We'd started at 8p.m. Two hours later he was still denying everything and taking the piss with smart-arse answers and a permanent smile.

"You can't do nothing. 'Cause I've got nothing to do with any tart's death," he says stabbing a finger across the table at me.

A picture of a girl not connected with Farmer pops into my head. My niece, Nicola. Eighteen, dead from a drugs overdose shot between her toes because she hadn't any other viable veins left. Just lying on a divan in her halls of residence at uni with dried vomit on her chin and streaks of it on her blue T-shirt. I try very hard to not let it get in the way and hang onto my temper. But it's not working.

"Nothing, you hear me" and he spells out the word N-O-T-H-I-N-G.

I can feel myself seriously wanting to wipe the smile off his face.

"You're rubbish, Joey, I'm going to put you …"

"N-O-T-H-I-N-G."

"You'll be an old man when you come out."

"N-O-T-H-I-N-G."

"That's if you ever come out."

"N-O-T-H-I-N-G."

I look at my watch.

"Interview terminated at 10.14 p.m."

I switched off the tape. And this time dealing with this kind of human rubbish that hadn't a thought about the lives they ruined or the families' anguish in the aftermath was just once too often and something snapped. I hit him almost before I realised it. The look on his face as he went over backwards was of complete and absolute surprise. When he landed, his mouth was bleeding. I bent down and grabbed him up by his shirt. The blows rained in, turning his face red. His nose exploded with blood even though the other DC with me was pulling me away.

The room filled with Joey shouting, then the alarm. I couldn't make out what he was saying. All I could see were the lips that had burst, spouting blood where before they had been spurting ridicule, and the nose, broken, and the pain in his eyes. And then the custody sergeant and two PCs were on top of me. Joey spreadeagled, shirt and jacket bloodied, eyes closed. His body heaved as he took in air, but he didn't know much about it.

"No, I haven't forgotten Joey," I replied, "or how to do it. So you see, Bobby," I said, moving threateningly right up close, "you're better off with some dough from me than me and a couple of my mates finishing what Stafford started the other day."

He stroked his chin nervously.

"Oi, Bobby!" someone called. We turned around to find a tall bald-headed chap in shirt and tie beckoning him over to the pay counter window. "You retired or something?"

Bobby lifted a hand.

"Five minutes, right!"

He led me to an alley at the back of the shop. It was small and enclosed. It smelt of piss and rubbish from the dustbins. You could see the lights of the betting shop through the back door's barred and grimy windows. It was quiet except for the swish of the wind blowing leaves and sweet wrappers in the narrow roadway.

"What's this about five hundred quid?" he asked.

"I want to know about Frank Harvey."

"What about him?"

"Did he plot up the Weindenfeldt raid?"

Bobby cleaned his fingernails with a matchstick and said nothing. I repeated the question, then picked up a dustbin lid and banged it hard back on the dustbin. The sound bounced from wall to wall and around the alley. You could tell it had startled him. Truth be told all that noise startled me a bit.

"I asked you a question."

"Frank did most of the planning," he said hastily, "then roped Don in. Me and Don was good mates. They needed someone to deal with the safe in case there was any aggro with it. So Don put me in it."

"And George?"

"Frank wanted George 'cause George likes breaking heads. We weren't keen 'cause he's got a reputation for shooting his gob off. But Frank insisted. You didn't argue with Frank." He finished cleaning his nails and flicked the match across the alley.

"And Terry?"

"We needed a wheel man. George wanted his brother. Terry's nothing without George. A lot of this" and he motioned his hand like an opening and closing mouth, "but he's a shit-hot driver."

"What happened? At the getaway, I mean."

"The job went sweet as a nut. But a taxi clipped us as we was taking off, accidental like. Don got out the motor absolutely barking. He had a lunatic temper at the best of times. I once saw him beat up a bloke who'd held a shop door open for his missus 'cause Don thought the geezer was trying to pull her. We're talking mental, right! Anyway, he started shouting and screaming at the cabby. Then this copper come from nowhere, absolutely nowhere, and the next thing you know Don's in the kerb, claret everywhere."

"All for nothing!"

"He didn't have to have got out the motor. Another half a minute Terry would have had us away."

"I meant Frank legging it with the gear. Then getting caught."

Bobby brushed imaginary dust off his jacket then hitched his sleeves back up to his elbows.

"I reckon you've had a good five hundred's worth, don't you?"

"Not quite!"

"You're not winding me up about this dough, are you?"

"How'd Frank get on with his missus?"

He pulled a fag out of his jacket and lit up, then smiled.

"Old prim and proper Lisa! Well, prim and proper Lisa was having it off with someone and Frank's only gone and hired some iffy enquiry agent to follow her."

I could see Lisa at the funeral in my mind's eye, crying and distraught, hardly able to bring herself to believe Frank was dead. Another picture of us at the house, her looking lovingly at Frank's photo and now here was Bobby telling me she had someone on the side.

"Who was the enquiry agent?" Bobby shrugged. "Name and address or no dough!"

"What happens if I can't get it?"

"You will."

He looked at his watch, a gold job with a black crocodile strap, but not as good as my Rolex, which for all his declarations about going straight he couldn't have afforded unless it was bent.

"I've got to get back. I'll be in touch."

I gave him my card.

"You do that. I'm in the Yellow Pages if you lose it, under 'E'. Right between Embalmers and Environmental Pest Control. Oh! There's one other thing."

"You don't want much for your money, do you?"

"Your mate, Don. D'you know where his widow lives?"

"I used to; we've lost touch."

"I'll have her address as well."

"There's nothing else is there? The safe keys, a date with Kate Moss?"

"No thanks, I've already got a girlfriend; anyway she's not my type."

He walked up the alley, his jacket collar up, his shoulders hunched. He turned the corner without looking back and disappeared. I followed him to see how my nag had done.

CHAPTER 13

I stood in a doorway opposite Leyton's shop in Queensway. A light rain blew in the wind. It was nearly 8 p.m. Saxone was late. Queensway was busy even at this time of night. It heaved with strollers, shoppers, singles, couples, old, young with a variety of languages, and no wonder practically every other shop was a restaurant or takeaway offering French, German, Italian or Chinese cuisine. The wet road and pavements bathed with the reflections of their neon lights and the lights from the traffic. More importantly though, were lights shining through the long casement windows of Leyton's flat above his shop.I checked my watch again.I'd told Saxone 7.30 p.m.I wondered if it had been such a good idea to bring him along. The plan was we'd ring Leyton's door and tell him we were police. I thought it would look better if there were two of us, then we'd show him something resembling warrant cards. 'We'll get answers from him all right' I could hear Saxone saying in my mind, 'you'll see, I promise you' and he'd laughed that sickly, fawning little laugh of his and now it was nearly 8 p.m. I decided I'd waited long enough.

I rang the bell. Nothing. I rang again. The door opened and there stood Brian Saxone. It took a second or two to register. I was about to ask what the hell his game was when he grabbed me and pulled me inside.

"Sorry, laddie, I got here earlier than I expected."

"Where's Leyton?"

He jerked his thumb upwards.

"He's just about to sing."

We walked down a long carpeted corridor. A draught blew across my legs and whistled off somewhere. We went upstairs.

56

"In here," Saxone said. "You're going to love this, Eddie, absolutely love it!"

The room was large and had white painted walls and thick beige carpeting. Up one end, beside a mock Adam-style fireplace were several rows of bookshelves stacked to the gunnels and dotted around the room a couple of leather winged armchairs. But it wasn't the fireplace or the books that grabbed your attention. It was the middle-aged man in the middle of the room, his wrists strapped to the arms of a chair.

"Mister Leyton. This is my associate, Mister … well, let's just say my associate," Saxone said.

Leyton hunched forward, his eyes dark and sunken into a craggy lined face that was greyish-white and wore the haunted look that people wear when they're anticipating a great deal of pain. The man, the chair, the scene had just registered when I noticed a small black box on the carpet with a white dial on it. There was a wire out of one end into an electrical socket and two wires out of the other end. Saxone picked up the two and held them towards Leyton.

"How much did you fence the jewellery for?"

Ralph leaned right back in his chair. He tried to gesticulate with his hands. But of course, he couldn't. Strands of his thin grey hair fell on his forehead. Beads of sweat ran off his temple and soaked into his shirt collar.

I grabbed Saxone's arm and said I wanted a word outside. He turned to Leyton and told him he'd be back in a minute and not to go anywhere.

"What the hell's going on?" I asked as we stepped onto the landing. "I thought we were supposed to be meeting outside."

"A change of plan."

"And what's all this crap with your do-it-yourself ECG kit?"

"You're going to …"

"I know, I'm going to love it."

"It's simple. The ends of the wires are live. I just give him a little shock treatment to wake his memory up."

I could have told him about a couple of guys I knew from the East End who used to collect debts with one of those things. They'd abduct their victims. Put them in a wheelie bin with a locking frame over it to scare them shitless to start with. Drive to a lock-up near Epping Forest. Then go to work on them. That was until one victim had had a coronary. And now they're doing ten apiece for manslaughter in Brixton. I grabbed Saxone's arm and asked what he'd do if Leyton keeled over?

"Don't worry. I haven't killed anyone yet."

"Jesus! You mean you've used this before!"

"Oh yes! You get all the information you want by the time the dial's at three."

He broke loose of my grip and went back inside. I followed him and stood beside the plug ready to yank it if things got heavy. Leyton was sweating hard now. It ran down the side of his face and dampened his shirt with a spreading stain. And then there appeared another across the front of his trousers. And I thought that at any moment he was going to shit himself. Steve was right. He probably was sixty-ish. But right now he looked eighty.

"I don't know anything. Honest," he was saying.

"Well, we're just going to shake your memory a bit," Saxone said. He pinched Leyton's nostrils together and as Leyton opened his mouth shoved some ragging in it and slapped some tape over it.

The two East End debt collectors stuck their victims' feet in buckets of water for added effect. But even without water there was no way Leyton would beat the dial. I gave him a minute, two at the most before he told Saxone everything.

"We just pull the switch like this," Saxone said nonchalantly as though he was boiling a kettle. Leyton's eyes, which had dilated to the size of marbles, stared at the box. He shook his head and mumbled something, but the gag and the tape muffled it. Saxone turned the dial up and a flat nasty menacing hum from the box filled the room. Leyton tried to struggle free but there was as much chance of that as there was of persuading Saxone not to go ahead. He held the two wires out and let them briefly touch. They crackled violently as a blue spark jumped between them. "Just bang your feet when you want to speak, Mister Leyton." He turned the dial down. The hum died but the threat lingered. "Well, you asked for it, Ralphy." He slipped the box towards the chair and stood behind Leyton, then brushed one of the wires against the old man's neck keeping the other one out of contact. "Sure you've got nothing to say?"

Leyton shook his head. Saxone grazed the wire against his neck again.

"Sure?" Waited a moment then made contact with the second wire. The hair on Ralph's neck suddenly stood up as his head started vibrating. His breathing, which hadn't sounded too great anyway, became heavy and erratic as he pumped air in and out of his nostrils. I made a move for the plug, but Saxone had withdrawn the wires. Leyton slumped sideways. His eyes full of misery.

"That was three seconds," Saxone said. "If you feel bad, Ralphy, remember I haven't even really started yet. You'll need a three-month holiday to get over the next lot."

You could tell Ralph was a beaten man. It was written across his lined face. I knew it, Saxone knew it. So I wondered how much of the act was meant to psych the victim and how much just violence. More violence than psych, I thought, as well as thinking this wasn't how I understood insurance investigators did their job. In fact, I could hardly believe what I was seeing.

"Anything to tell me, Ralph, about ten million pounds' worth of jewellery?" Leyton was silent. "Oh well, seconds out, round two." He turned the dial up. The box hummed again. He let it resonate for a moment to let Ralph know how bad things could get, then turned the dial back to two. He pressed both wires against Leyton's ear.

They'd barely touched when Leyton thrashed about and stamped his feet. Saxone pulled the wires away and ripped the tape off his mouth.

"I'll tell you, I'll tell you, please stop!" Leyton cried.

"Okay, so how d'you come to fence the Weindenfeldt stuff?"

"He came to me one day. Frank, that is, and another man just before I was closing the shop. He said he'd be getting about ten million pounds' worth of jewellery, was I interested and could I handle that amount?"

"Two of them?" Saxone asked.

"Yes."

He asked him about the other man. His name, a description, accent, scars. But Leyton couldn't help. Saxone even threatened him with more wire. But he just couldn't recall.

"Would you know him again if you saw him?" Saxone asked.

"Maybe."

"Okay, so the two of them propositioned you; what then?"

"I'd done business with Harvey before, rings, necklaces, diamonds from time to time, good stuff, untraceable. So I knew I could do business with him."

I asked Leyton if he had any drink. He said behind me. I opened a small Regency cabinet and with a pair of thin white latex gloves I always carried with me withdrew a bottle of Martell and three glasses. I poured three shots and passed the first to Saxone, expecting him to feed it to Ralph, but he knocked it back himself. I gave him a look and then fed the second to Leyton. He spluttered a bit but got it down.

"So what was the deal?" Saxone asked.

"A million for the gear."

"You greedy bastard!" he snarled and slapped Leyton. His head jerked and for a moment I thought he'd topple backwards.

"How d'you pay him? Cash?" He didn't reply. "How!" Saxone demanded.

"With two banker's drafts," Leyton spat.

Nice one, I thought. Banker's drafts, cheques as good as cash that can't be stopped and can be exchanged for cash sterling almost anywhere in the world.

"At first Frank wouldn't have it. He wanted cash. I told him no one was going to seriously put a million quid in a suitcase. I mean, think of the risk. Besides …"

"Besides what!" Saxone demanded. Leyton hesitated. "Besides what?" Saxone shouted.

"It legitimised everything our end."

"How d'you mean?"

"I'm connected with a diamond company in Brussels that deal in stolen stuff. They send me the drafts, via their offices in Hatton Garden. Once I'm satisfied with the gear I hand over the drafts for the goods. Then I pass the stuff to Hatton Garden together with an invoice from a dummy company in Liechtenstein for a million pounds. The Brussels people then have a receipt for their outlay. They take a million pounds' worth of jewellery from the parcel, re-cut and re-set the stones to disguise them. So they now have stock to support the invoice plus nine million pounds' worth of jewellery to trade secretly for cash, which may bring them in four or five million under the counter. And nobody bats an eyelid either here or in Belgium, because for a diamond company dealing in millions of pounds a year, issuing two half- mil drafts is nothing."

You had to hand it to the old bastard. It was some stroke! I looked over at Saxone. The look on his face had changed. It took me a moment or two to realise what it was. Even he was beginning to respect this piece of villainy.

"In the end Frank and his partner agreed. I suppose on the basis, that if they got turned over, they knew where I lived. Also I think because they were going abroad."

I asked him why he thought that.

"Because," he continued, "when I repeated that the drafts were as good as money and saved dragging a suitcase of cash everywhere, they came round to the idea."

I could see the sense. You get challenged and asked to open your bags at customs; you could hardly say you'd stopped off at an ATM. And abroad would be their only option once the double-cross was revealed.

"And what did you get out of it?" Saxone asked.

"Ten per cent of the drafts' value paid separately by Belgium." He looked at me and said. "You blokes going to kill me now I've told you all this?"

"Not unless you'd like us to." Saxone undid one of the straps. "No one's going to kill you. You're not worth the effort." He pulled the strap free, unplugged his toy and said, "Wait ten minutes, then undo the other strap. Understand?" Leyton nodded. Saxone wiped his own glass of prints and then for good measure smashed it underfoot on the carpet. And then we were out of there.

CHAPTER 14

Saxone suggested we go back to his place in Shepherd's Bush for a drink as it wasn't far. I followed him in my car through wet empty streets streaked with the watery reds and yellows of shop lights. His place was a huge first-floor flat in a conversion of three in Caxton Street. He showed me into the living room, a beautiful, twenty-odd-foot, cream embossed wallpaper affair with restored ceiling mouldings and a wonderful original ceiling rose from which hung a large crystal chandelier. He pointed to a beige moquette sofa that was so comfortable it felt as though you were sitting on a cloud.

"Scotch?"

"Don't ever pull a stunt like that on me again."

"Leyton, right?"

"Never! Got it!"

"Tetchy, aren't we. Don't worry about the old bampot, he's nothing."

"Never! Got it! You know I'm getting very bad vibes about you."

"What's your problem? That it was me, not you, that discovered we're not looking for jewellery any more, but banker's drafts?"

"Your methods."

"Well, tut!, tut!, matey. You do what you have to. That's how you get results."

I wondered how far he would go. 'Doing what you have to' can justify anything. I run close to the wind myself. But I wouldn't knowingly run the risk of killing someone and pass it off as being all in a day's work. He handed me a Scotch in an exquisite crystal cut whisky glass and said,

"Think I'm wrong, do you? Well, I bet the police or the two Nortons wouldn't mind knowing what we two know."

"What we four know."

"Pardon me?"

"What we four know. There's you and me, and Ralph, and Frank's partner."

"If there was one."

"There was."

"How d'you know?"

"Lisa told me."

"You mean you knew about this?"

"Not about the drafts."

"You cunning little bastard! What else did she tell you?"

It started raining again. You could hear thunder rolling. Then a streak of white lightning split the inky blue night, all so vivid being up so high. I mulled over who could be Frank's partner and came to the obvious — George, Terry or Bobby. Frank had been some player. He'd picked the target, planned the raid, lined up a fence, copped the jewellery, and made safe arrangements to leave the country, because he knew all the time he'd planned to double-cross the others. Industrialised crime. So, who would someone like that choose for a partner?

"Well, Sutton, what else did she tell you?"

"That Frank was attacked by someone on his way back from Ralph's that Saturday night, presumably because they believed he'd be carrying the fenced cash."

He went to the window and just stared at the night.

"Jesus! D'you know who?"

"His partner, I suppose."

"I've got an idea," he said at last. "Why don't I bug the Nortons' and Hallet's phones? See what turns up."

"Bug them! Are you serious?"

"Absolutely, laddie, whatever it takes. Never ignored the rule book?"

There was another crack of thunder and rain beat against the windows. I couldn't tell if it was a straight question, or he knew about my past. Of course he did! He'd have had me checked out.

"Well, haven't you?"

"Haven't I what?"

"Ignored the rule book and taken the law into your own hands?"

"I suppose so."

"Well, there you are!" he said holding out his glass in a mock toast. "You wanna lighten up!"

I finished my drink. He asked if I wanted another. I said no because I didn't want one and wanted to be out of his company.

It was still raining hard. It bounced on the windscreen and made jagged and distorted patterns of the street lights, and in between them I could see Leyton's misery-ridden face.

CHAPTER 15

The drive to Crouch End took about thirty minutes. I sat looking at the house. Even though I'd rung in advance I checked for Henry's car. No car meant no Henry.

"How are you?" I kissed her and closed the door behind us, holding her close.

"Henry's back."

"Where is he?"

"In the garden shed."

"What!"

She wrinkled her little nose that sat so snugly between high cheekbones The only blemish on it, two tiny red marks where her glasses, when she wore them, sat. Her smile started from the lips and eased its way across her face. Then two dimples appeared and the smile was complete.

"Joke! He's in Manchester, at some exhibition."

I pulled her closer slipping my hand down her knickers, feeling that lovely bowling ball of an arse. She slapped my hand.

"Naughty detective! Here, let me look at you. It's been so long since I saw you. I need to be sure who's groping me."

"Two days."

"Three. But who's counting."

"I rang you. Once, I got voicemail, the second time you were engaged."

"You should have tried a third time."

I followed her into the kitchen. She stirred a cup of percolated coffee. She asked if I wanted. She wore a long pink T-shirt that finished halfway down her legs. At thirty-six she still had a great figure and great legs. She poured me a cup. Strands of her hair, not

66

quite secured by a small plastic comb, fell on her neck, brown on pink. She carried the two cups into the living room, a blue Regency-striped wallpaper affair with reproduction furniture. She set them down on a coffee table and sat beside me on the sofa.

"You won't be able to stay long."

"Oh!"

"Kathy, Henry's sister, is coming over with some dresses from a catalogue thing she's into. She's ringing before she comes."

"Pity."

"So, what's new, lover boy? Why haven't I seen you for nearly a week?"

"I'm working on a case."

"Hmm, you and your cases."

"What does hmm mean?"

"All those shitty people with their shitty problems."

"And their shitty cheques when I solve them."

"You should get a real job."

"I got a real job and a real woman."

"Hmmm" was all she said.

I pulled her close and kissed her, feeling her breasts squash against me as her tongue found the inside of my mouth.

"I'm glad you called," she whispered. "I miss you. I miss you a lot. I've been thinking about you."

I eased her out of her T-shirt and bra and began licking her nipples.

"Don't. You know what that does to me."

I licked some more.

"What does it do, Rita? What does it do to you?"

"This." She unzipped my flies.

I was hardly out of my trousers when she knelt down in front of me. She took me in her mouth slowly at first, running the flat part of her tongue up and down, watching me lose my mind.

"See what you could be having every night, Eddie darling?" she whispered so softly I could just about hear her. "Every night,

Eddie. Whenever you wanted it. Wherever you wanted it. In bed, on the bed, on the floor, in the shower, because I know how you like to do it in the shower."

My blood which was jumping around inside my veins jumped some more.

She went back to the job in hand, so to speak. But faster, her head bobbing like a continual yes to an unasked question, her face almost hidden by her hair that had fallen free of the comb. When she'd decided she'd just about rattled my brain, she slid on top of me slowly, but knowing exactly what she was doing.

"Oh, you feel so good, Eddie! Real good!" She clasped her hands around my neck. She bit my lip and drew blood, then sank her teeth into my shoulder and drew blood again. "So, so good," she said in such a low voice I couldn't tell if the words were meant for me or herself. She filled herself with me gyrating side to side then back and forth. She put my fingers in her mouth one at a time, sucking and licking, then three of them together. "Oh, so, so very good for little Rita." Her breath suddenly came hard and sharp. She grabbed my hair and pulled me towards her. "Oh, Eddie! E-D-D-I-E!" But Eddie wasn't listening any more, because Eddie was busy getting done himself.

She lay back on the sofa, her eyes closed, her breathing easing. Both of us enjoying the silence. And then the phone rang. The sound of it completely filling the room.

"Sod it!" she exclaimed, her eyes still closed. "It'll be Kathy."

"Let it ring."

"She knows I'm in." She reached over and answered. "Kathy, sure, half an hour's fine." She replaced the receiver and said 'sod it' again. "Sorry, baby, you're out of here."

We kissed at the door. She held me tightly and brushed her hand against my face.

"How I hate all this."

"All what?"

"This. You and me. Episodes. I just want us to be together all the time."

"We're okay, aren't we?"

Her face was flushed from the sex, but her eyes were sad.

"You know, my mum and dad were married when they were in their twenties and they still absolutely adore each other. I mean they absolutely love each other to pieces. That's all I ever wanted. To be like them. To make a home for myself with a man who I really loved. Cook, have friends round to dinner. What's wrong with that, Eddie?"

"Nothing, I suppose."

"Exactly. Nothing. It's not a lot to ask of life, is it? Eight years is a long time to be married to the wrong man. I won't settle for a life with Henry. I want to be part of a real couple and grow old with the right someone."

"And that's me, is it?"

She looked at me and smiled.

"You'd do. Oh, you'd do very well, Mister Sutton." I pulled her to me and put my arms around her. "I'm just an ordinary girl, Eddie. I left school and became a secretary. But all I ever wanted to do was get married and have a family. I made a mistake through my haste. But I'm not one for compounding my mistakes. Ring me, Eddie."

"Tomorrow, I promise." I kissed her and drove home.

CHAPTER 16

I awoke with a start the next morning from a dream about a Nazi dressed up as an insurance investigator interrogating an old man. He made notes on the back of a banker's draft. The Nazi would smile, fold the draft in half and half again and then it would disappear. I thought about Brian Saxone, and the more I thought, the less I liked him. Last night had been brutal. If I hadn't been there, chances are Ralph would have got a good hiding on top of everything else.

I thought about Rita while showering. She wanted marriage or at least to live with me. I'd lived with girlfriends before, a few times over the years. Somehow we'd never stayed together. Afraid of commitment, I suppose. Your whole lifestyle changes when you're under the same roof with someone. I have single friends. We like good West End bars. We like eyeing women, even if we don't always pull. We like good restaurants because we're not short of a bob or two. I like the impromptu decision to play cards and find myself still playing into the early hours with jazz in the background and a bottle of something, usually Scotch, not far away. I wondered how Rita would handle me waltzing in at 2 a.m. telling her I'd been playing poker with my mates. She was a good woman, sex was great, but ... I'd had all these thoughts before and it always ended up the same way, by me pushing everything to the back of my mind and thinking about something else. It was like that now. As I found myself thinking about Lisa and Frank's letter.

The Benidorm room was the Finsbury Park B&B. But what the hell was a spent wind and dishes and vodka and orange? I decided I needed another look at the letter, so I phoned her after my breakfast and arranged to see her. I'd just finished piling everything into the sink when Bobby Hallet rang.

"Re our chat," he said. He sounded a little nervous. The edge of self-assurance and cockiness he'd had the other day was missing. I asked if everything was all right. He said it was. But it didn't sound that way."I've come up with some names and addresses."

"I thought you might."

"Five hundred, you said."

"That's right." He wanted the dough first. But I told him after I had the info.

"The geezer what Frank hired is called Lenny Warren. He's got an office, first floor above a firm of estate agents called Henley Graham in Tottenham."

"Nice one! And Don's widow?"

"Her name's Susan." He gave me an address in Hackney.

The nervous edge crept back into his voice. I asked him again if he was okay.

"Fine. Why wouldn't I be! You in the market for more stuff?"

"Maybe. What you got?"

"I've been nosing around. There's more than meets the eye with this business. There's people who aren't what they seem."

"Meaning?" Lisa jumped to mind.

"First things first. When you weighing in with the dough?"

"Whenever suits."

He told me he had an errand to run in the West End the following day. So we fixed a meet at the Poland Street multi-storey car park for 4 p.m.

"Second floor. I'll be in a blue Escort van, all right?" and he gave me the registration number.

"What did you mean, there are people who aren't what they seem?"

"Just that, and they're taking the piss. We'll talk about it tomorrow," and he rang off.

71

Then I phoned Rita, who had a part-time secretarial job with a firm of accountants in Muswell Hill, and invited her out to dinner for the following evening.

It was just after 10.30 a.m. as I parked outside Lisa's. The kids from the other day were cycling in the roadway. I decided, kids or not, if any of them spat at the Beema today, political correctness or not, they'd get a mouthful from me and dragged round to their parents to let them know what kind of rubbish they were bringing up. Lisa said hello and led me upstairs. There were fresh roses in glass vases dotted around the living room that helped brighten up the place. She looked brighter too. The pasty white complexion of the other day had gone, replaced with some natural colour even though she wore blusher. She looked more relaxed as well. And it went through my mind again, because junior is always on the lookout, it was a shame she was so recently bereaved or else who knows? Nice face, lovely figure, thirty-something, shame to let it all go to waste.

"How's the investigation going?" she asked.

"I'd like to have another look at Frank's personal prison effects."

She brought the things in from the bedroom and laid them carefully on the coffee table. I held each of the paperbacks by its cover and shook it.

"What you doing?" she asked.

"Looking for Frank's dough."

"Come again!" I told her of my chat with Ralph. "That's brilliant!" she exclaimed. Then after a moment's thought said, "But that means they could be anywhere."

"'Fraid so!"

There was nothing in the books. I broke the handles of the hairbrush and the toothbrush and a safety razor in case they were hollow. But I needn't have bothered; a copper's instinct told me the drafts were still at the B&B. That left the letter. Frank had had a coronary. He thought he might die. It stood to reason that all the reminiscing crap about Benidorm and the drink had to be his way of telling her where he'd hidden the drafts. I reread the letter to her. About his heart, their holiday, the hotel, her drink. But none of it still made any sense. Lisa was still in black. Black shirt, black tights, black sweater; she was in mourning. Yet Bobby said she had someone on the side.

"It don't make sense," she said.

"No, it doesn't," I replied. "You sure you've never been to Benidorm or drunk vodka and orange?"

"Oi, what d'you take me for! Course I am."She got a pad and pencil and printed the words vodka and orange along one half of the page and Benidorm on the other and tried to make word associations with the two. "He ever hardly wrote, and when he does I can't bloody understand what 'e's trying to say."

We spent a little longer on what Frank might have meant by it all including dishes that weren't dishes and winds and so on. But we didn't get anywhere. I had a cup of coffee and decided to pay Lenny Warren a visit.

"If you think of anything, anything at all, ring me," I said as she walked me to the door. She smiled. She looked good when she smiled, really good.

"D'you think the wind and the dishes and the drink and all that stuff's really got something to do with the money, Eddie?"

"Yes."

"So do I." She pecked me on the cheek and said she'd ring.

"Frank's trying to tell you where the drafts are. You knew him better than anyone else. Keep thinking!"

CHAPTER 17

The sign on the door said L Warren & Associates but, standing there on the other side of his desk, I wondered who'd want to associate with him. He was in his late forties. The grey at his temples was on the move. His suit needed pressing, so did he.

"My name's Eddie Sutton; I called earlier."

"Yeah!" He offered me a seat and gave me a lavish smile from a long bony face. It was a business smile without sincerity that came from force of habit. "So what can I do for you?"

"I'm after some information."

"Is that a fact!"

"We're in the same business you and me, Mister Warren. We have mutual acquaintances."

"Who's that then?"

"Frank Harvey."

"I only know one Frank Harvey. It wouldn't be him."

"Scrubbs. On remand for armed robbery in the July that's just gone. Died a fortnight ago."

He looked at me his eyes nearly squinting, crow's feet appearing at the corners, hard experienced eyes taking in every detail.

"Got any other mutual acquaintances?" he asked.

"Don Taylor," I lied.

"How is Don?"

"Dead as well."

"Your friends don't live long, do they."

"That's why I don't have many."

"Been in this line long?" he asked.

"Long enough."

He opened a desk drawer and pulled out a Yellow Pages and asked, "How's business?"

"Up and down. Like a whore's drawers."

"Well, well, so you are!" He ran a nicotined finger across the page. "E Sutton, Enquiry Agent and Certified Court Bailiff." He snapped the book shut and dropped it on the floor. Dust rose from the carpet. "You'd be surprised the stories I've heard from that chair, Mister Sutton. So, you need information?"

I looked around the room. Bare except for essentials like the wooden desk between us, two grey filing cabinets in the corner and the black PVC chairs we sat on. I compared the starkness of his office with the comfort of mine. The expensive wooden flooring, comfortable Habitat chairs, soft lighting. I like to live well, surround myself with nice things. If people come to an office that gives off successful vibes, they're more likely to have confidence in you. Even if you're the biggest klutz in the world, which I'm not. I decided Lenny Warren liked money. But didn't like spending it.

"There'd be a drink in it for you."

"I should hope so! What d'you need to know?"

"If Frank hired you to find out if his missus had a bloke on the side."

"Who told you she might?"

"A friend of Don's."

"And what's your interest?"

I laid five twenties on his desk.

"Yes or no? And don't lie or I'll be back for a refund if you know what I mean!"

He stretched his hand across and took the money.

"I don't give refunds! But you'd be welcome to try. If you know what I mean!" he said coolly, matter-of-factly like he knew he could back it up. "The answer's no. I was never hired by Frank to follow his wife."

"I do hope you're telling me the truth." I buttoned my Armani jacket, finding myself quite pleased that Lisa was legit and wasn't taking the piss. As for Bobby, he and I would be having a few words! "Nice to have met you, Mister Warren."

"But I was hired to follow someone."

"Don't mess me around. Who?"

He rubbed his finger and thumb.

"That's another oner."

I dropped back in the chair and stared at him wondering if he wasn't just hustling. I was tempted to grab hold of him and give him a shaking except something told me he'd shake back and that wouldn't help.

"Okay, who?"

"In advance!"

"You know you'd make Shylock blush!"

"Who's that, another one of your friends?"

"This better be good, Warren."

"Don hired me to follow his wife."

"Susan!"

"He phoned me a few weeks before he died. We had a meet in a pub in Islington, the Silver Fox. He reckoned Susan was having it off with some geezer and he wanted me to get the SP."

"And was she?"

"Oh, she was having it off, all right, left and centre! I followed her two afternoons. She'd meet him in a car park. Not with a 'oh, fancy meeting you here' kiss. But an 'I really got the hots for you' kind."

I wondered how he knew about a 'hots for you' kind of kiss. Because I couldn't imagine anyone having the hots for him.

"Where did they go?"

"To a flat both times."

"His?"

"I don't know. I was doing a friend a favour for a drink. I just took a couple of snaps of them together and sent it to Don."

"Can you describe him?"

"Leave it out!" He thought for a moment, then said, "Tall, no, medium height, drove a big, sleek car."

"What type?"

Warren shrugged.

"You don't want much for your hundred quid, do you?"

"Two hundred, but who's counting."

"I don't remember. It wasn't exactly one of my major cases." He yawned and as he stretched said, "It's lucky for her and her boyfriend Don died. He wasn't one to let his wife get up to hanky-panky without doing something about it."

"Talking of photos. D'you think you might have kept a copy?"

He stretched back in his chair supporting his head with laced fingers. The bony face broke into a smile.

"Unlikely. Even if I did it wouldn't be here."

"Where then?"

"I keep all old files at Swinburn's in Islington, the archive security people, otherwise if anyone ever broke in here they'd have a field day with some of the stuff I've been involved with. If there is a copy, it'll be with them, probably in a miscellaneous file of odds and ends for 2012 or 2013." I asked him if he'd check it out. "The thing is, Mister Sutton, time is money. I've got to ring them, and they got to search out the year or years, which they'll charge me for …"

"You're breaking my heart!" I took out another oner and left it on his desk.

"What's your mobile number? I'll let you know, but don't hold your breath."

I buttoned my jacket for the second time and said I expected to hear from him in the next couple of days.

CHAPTER 18

Rita was right on time at Camden Town tube looking really sexy in a clinging shirt and blue mini. We went to an Indian restaurant near me, then back to my place. We lay on the sofa in each other's arms. The lights were low, Eva Cassidy oozed very softly from the hi-fi in the corner of the room. I started unbuttoning her Valentino shirt. The bra was lacy and covered too much; my fingers found the clasp.

"I've got something to tell you," she whispered. "I'm leaving Henry."

Her words hung there. It takes a lot to distract me when I'm undressing a woman; I'm very single-minded during such things. But that did it.

"You sure you're not doing anything hasty, Reet?"

"I should have done it ages ago."

"Where will you stay?" I could have bitten my tongue off as soon as the words were out of my mouth.

"Well," she began.

"And what about money?" I asked, hoping to derail the answer to the first question.

"Money won't be a problem. I'm going back to work full-time. As for a place, it depends." And you didn't need three guesses or have to phone a friend to know on what.

"But divorce, it's a big step, Reet."

"There's nothing between me and Henry. The marriage has been bad for ages. You know that."

"But divorce! I think you should put off telling him for a while."

"Why?"

78

"Because, because …"

The end of the sentence was interrupted by the front-door buzzer, long urgent rings that couldn't be ignored.

"Bloody hell! It's 10.30 p.m.," she exclaimed. "It's not business surely."

"It better not be."

"This is just the sort of thing I mean about your work."

I pressed the entryphone and asked who it was. A voice said,

"Police, open up."

I decided to go downstairs instead of just buzzing them up, because of the time of night. I hurried down and along the passage, the flooring cold under my feet. The buzzer rang again. I'd half-opened it when something hit me on the nose. I tried to slam the door shut but it was shoved back with such force that I was pushed backwards. I lashed out a fist as I stumbled, but I just connected with thin air. Then something hit me on the side of the head, making everything dreamlike and unreal except the nausea in my guts. That was real. There seemed to be two of them, but through my watery vision everything was just a rough fluid outline, a swirl of greys and blacks moving quickly and making a din. Someone grabbed me by the hair and pulled me backwards. The nausea was momentarily forgotten, replaced by the pain from someone pulling my scalp from my head. Street instinct made me drop my hands to protect the meat and two veg as the other one hit me in the guts. From a long way off I could hear Rita calling, then someone screaming; everything blurred as I felt myself being dragged upstairs.

I shook my head to clear the fog, but the fog was in no hurry to move. Someone slapped my face and said I'd be all right. But he wasn't lying where I was with a head that felt three times its normal size. I opened my eyes properly. There were two of them, George Norton and a black guy about six foot with small bad uneven teeth, hair cropped to the scalp and built like a brick shithouse. I'd fallen for one of my own tricks of opening the front door because someone said they were the police. I looked for Rita, who sat in the corner of the room, her face as white as the shirt she wore.

"I wanna have a word with you," George yelled.

I started to get up but the schvatze put a shoe on my chest.

"You been causing me a lot of bovva. I don't like that. So I've come round to sort it." He picked up a table lamp and looked at it for a moment. "Nice place you got here. Real smart," he said, then smashed the lamp against the coffee table showering the carpet with fragments. Rita gasped and almost jumped out of the sofa.

George's help pulled me up off the floor and slammed me against the wall. I was about to give him a good hard kick in the crotch when George pulled a razor. It stopped me dead. My mind emptied of everything. All I saw was the steel in those fat pork sausage-like fingers. I thought twice about the kick. Getting a few lumps and bumps or a bleeding nose was one thing, having your face sliced was something else. I could see from the corner of my eye Rita had grabbed a cushion, her fingers tightly curled around it as she clutched it to her breasts. She held it there for a moment, then started chewing the corner of it.

"We definitely gotta get this bit of trouble sorted, Sutton," George said. He snatched the cushion from Rita and slowly stroked the razor across it. The blade cut into the fabric and a shower of yellow and green foam crumbs fell out and settled over the fragments of the table lamp like coloured snow. "I told you to keep your nose out of things, didn't I? Seems you can't take advice. So now I'm gonna show you what happens. But first I wanna know what you know about this business?"

I wondered how to play it. Lie, half-lie, bullshit, but the blade focused my mind for me.

"There's not a lot to tell." My mouth was dry. I gulped but could command no saliva. George gave the cushion a second slice. The sound of the fabric ripping sent a shiver the length of my back.

"I'm running out of cushion, Sutton," he said, then ran the blunt side of the razor down the side of my face from temple to jaw slowly so you could feel the cold metal against flushed damp skin. The hair on my neck stood on end as the steel was moved to my chin.

I tried to move my head backwards, but pinned against the wall there was no backwards to go to. The schvatze smiled. He and George had done this before, you could tell, and they liked the work. Rita gasped, and burst into tears. I wanted to comfort her, but couldn't do anything.

"Cut it out, darling," George growled, "or I'll really give you something to bawl about." She pulled a tissue from her sleeve and dabbed her eyes. "Ten seconds, Sutton, then your little tart over there gets some tram-lines."

"Frank Harvey was going to double-cross you," I blurted.

"He what?"

"He planned to split the proceeds fifty–fifty with a mate instead of five ways with the gang and then the two of them were going to do a runner." I said it so quickly with such force that at the end of it I hardly had a breath left in my body. I expected surprise. I expected George to think on it, but all he said was,

"You taking the piss!"

"Who was your fence? If it wasn't Ralph Leyton, you were double-crossed. Frank set up a deal with him. All you'd have got was a postcard from Cyprus."

There was still no surprise. But George was now thinking on it all right. The black guy tightened his grip on me, I could tell, itching to let one go in my face.

"And how d'you know all this?" George finally asked.

"I got it from Leyton, chapter and verse."

George walked to the French windows, that were ajar and looked down on the wide residential street. He stared into the black night for what seemed a long while without speaking. There was no way of knowing what ran through his mind. It could have been anything from cursing Frank, to wondering how he could best dispose of me and Rita. I was getting worried about the second possibility when another thought dropped into my head and started bouncing like a ping-pong ball. What if George was Frank's partner, what then?

"Does this Leyton geezer know who Frank's partner is?" he asked, running a hand through his long greasy hair.

"No."

"And he lives where?"

"He trades from a jeweller's in Queensway, and lives in the flat above."

"So it's just you and Leyton?"

"And Rita here," and then concerned he truly might have ideas of doing us in added, "Lisa Harvey, and a friend that came with me to Ralph's."

The sweat and the smell of my own fear still filled my nostrils. I could feel the back of my shirt so completely soaked that it cloyed to the wall. But my mind was clearing. If George was going to kill us, I wasn't going to make it easy for him. I'd shove the black guy off and ram George hard enough to push him through the window. Twenty feet down on the pavement spread like trifle, we'd see how he felt about things then. The black guy would go for me sure, and probably cream me, but it would be one on one. Then again, with George downstairs needing to be shovelled up, he might decide to cut his losses. Either way, that's what I decided to do. I braced myself, took a deep breath when George closed the razor and ordered the other guy to let go of me, which he did by shoving me halfway across the room so that I ended up on the sofa beside Rita. She reached out an icy shaking hand to hold mine.

"You're a very lucky man, Sutton" is all that George said to me and then told his playmate they were out of there.

82

I heard them on the stairs, their shoes on the passage, then the slam of the front door and, as I turned to Rita to comfort her and hold her close, I noticed my hands were shaking too.

"I thought they were going to kill us!" she screamed.

"No, that's just George!"

"Don't be so bloody funny. The man's a psychopath. Who is he; what's this about?"

I looked around the room, at the pieces of the table lamp and foam crumb strewn over the carpet. The hi-fi was still on. Eva Cassidy was singing 'Life Is Just A Bowl Of Cherries'. Rita started to get up, but her legs gave way and she fell back onto the sofa and burst out crying again.

"I thought they were going to kill us, Eddie," she shrieked. "I really thought I was going to die."

I reached over and held her in my arms. Her sobs came long and heavy.

"Sssh, everything's okay, Reet."

"I really thought …"

"Everything's okay. Let me deadlock the front door, fix us both a drink, then let's go to bed."

CHAPTER 19

I awoke the next morning with the sun streaming through the bedroom window, and ran a hand over my sandpapery chin. Scenes from the night before flashed in my mind's eye passing like frames of a film. George and his mate. Me pinned against the wall. Though I knew I was safe I felt my stomach knot. Rita stirred beside me, then woke.

"What's the matter?" she asked, alarmed.

"It's okay, everything's all right."

"I thought for a moment it was them again." She cuddled close like a child. "I've never been so scared, Eddie. Never. Not in all my life. Such cruel, cruel-looking men."

"Don't worry, it's over."

She propped herself on her elbows.

"D'you think they believed what you told them?"

"Maybe. Either way, Ralph'll get a visit. It means George will discover the stuff was fenced for drafts. Oh well, it can't be helped."

"Whatever! Still, it's not your problem any more, is it. If the police want to interview me tell them to make it at my work."

"You don't think I'm going to the law, do you? What d'you expect George to say? 'It's a fair cop, guv. You've got me bang to rights.'"

"But you're out of it now, aren't you?"

If I'd been more awake I'd have had a better answer. But it just came out.

"You're joking. I've got fifty grand riding on the deal."

"You're not going on with the case surely. Not after last night. Even fifty grand's not worth losing your life for."

I went to touch her, but she got out of bed and put on a dressing gown hanging on the door. "You are, aren't you? You could have been killed last night. We both could."

"But we weren't."

"You don't give a shit about anyone, do you?"

"Rita …"

She just stood there looking at me, her arms folded across her breasts making long narrow creases in the blue silk gown.

"I see now what I didn't see before, Eddie." She gathered up her clothes and went into the bathroom. She came out dressed. She had mascara on, but it couldn't soften the anger in her eyes.

"Tea or coffee?"

"Neither." She stood in the doorway putting on her jacket.

"Where are you going?"

"Home."

I offered her a lift, but she said she'd get a cab. I offered her breakfast, but she declined that too.

"Oh, come on, Reet, don't be upset. Wait until the job's over and we'll talk about things."

"Bye, Eddie!"

I heard her footsteps along the passage. They were slow, not like George's and his mate's. The front door opened, but slammed much harder than it had done with their exit.

I sat at the kitchen table with a cup of coffee. Maybe Rita was right. I was in deeper than was good for me. We could have been killed or taken serious damage. But something I'd said, and said by chance, had stopped George in his tracks. But what was it? And suppose I hadn't said it. I heard Rita in my head. She reminded me of what my mum used to say to my dad when, as a police constable, he'd been involved in a dangerous incident. Poor Rita. A nice straightforward uncomplicated woman, who just wanted to love someone and be loved, cook, and have friends round to dinner and all I did was give her grief just like my father with my mother before the accident that retired him and confined him to that shitty council flat where the four of us lived and where I was brought up. I recalled Lisa turfing all Frank's stuff out onto the coffee table saying, 'Not much to show for a life, is it.' What had I to show for mine? Money, a flat on the edge of the West End. But no wife, no children. My parents dead. Just a younger brother. Maybe it was time to put down roots. I could do a lot worse than Rita. A lot, lot worse. And then what happens happened. The idea of getting married and commitment got pushed to the back of my mind and I thought about George and the case.

CHAPTER 20

I parked outside the house. I wondered whether to ring or take George's advice and call it a day. He'd scared me and twelve hours on my shoulder still hurt from the black guy pinning me against the wall. But I checked the house number and rang the bell. A kiddy's voice yelled out, "Mummy, Mummy" and seconds later the door opened. She was in her middling thirties, with long ash-blond hair that started in a fringe and ended on her shoulders, large green eyes with just the slightest squint in one of them.

"Mrs Taylor?"

The eyes picked me clean from face to crotch and back again. She smiled. It was perfunctory, it nevertheless lit her face making her look quite, quite pretty.

"No one here by that name."

"Susan Taylor, Don's missus."

The door opened wider and a kiddy clutching a doll popped her head round.

"Who is it, Mummy?"

"Go inside, Tracey!"

"But, Mummy …"

"Inside now. Sorry, I can't help you, mate."

I stuck my foot in the door.

"I was told she lives here."

"Well, you was told wrong. Now d'you mind," she said, pointing at my shoe.

"Auntie Susie and Uncle Don don't live here," the kiddy said, waving the doll's arm at me.

"You're a copper, aren't you?"

"My name's Eddie Sutton."

"A copper, right?"

"No."

"Well, you're not here to see if we have a TV licence."

"I'm an enquiry agent."

"Enquiring about what?"

"I'm doing some work that involves Don Taylor and some pals of his."

"The aggro in Kensington, right?"

She looked me up and down again, in not such an aggressive manner and told me her name was Monica, Susan's sister.

"D'you have any identity?"

I showed her a business card, a legit one, my driving licence and a credit card.

She looked them over then invited me in, and told Tracey to go play in the other room. She led me through a small hall. Flicked quickly at her hair as she passed a mirror, and showed me into a large through living room where the Victoriana of the ceiling mouldings and window shutters met the twenty-first century head on with gold and blue wallpaper and chart sounds coming from a radio perched on a shelf. She asked why I wanted to speak to Susie.

"Just a chat."

"Chat about what?"

"This 'n' that. Can I have her address?"

She stood leaning against a wall, her arms folded across a very pleasantly filled casual blue shirt. She didn't speak for nearly a minute then said,

"I'm afraid Susie passed away a few weeks ago." Her bottom lip started quivering. "She, she …" She tried to keep control but the tears streamed down her cheeks. "She took a load of sleeping pills. They said through depression, what with Don and everything."

"I'm sorry. I had no idea."

"I hadn't heard from her for a couple of days, which was unusual, and she wasn't answering her phone. So I went over. I had a set of keys for her place, and she kept a set of mine, for emergencies like." She blew her nose. "I still have dreams about it every now and then. Me trying to wake her, then seeing the empty pill bottle."

I said how sorry I was again. I wondered why Bobby hadn't mentioned it. Perhaps he didn't think I'd follow it up. Or more likely thought it might queer his five hundred quid.

She explained how she and her husband had wanted Susan to live with them so she shouldn't be on her own after Don's death. But Susan wouldn't.

"That's Bill, my husband, in the photo over there," she said pointing to some wedding snaps. There she was a few years ago, slightly thinner beside a tall, slim, round-faced chap standing nervously bolt upright who at twenty-six or -seven was balding. "It's the only photo he's ever had taken without darts or a pint in his hand. Anyway, you haven't told me what this is about. Not properly."

"I'm looking for the jewellery to return it to the insurers. I thought Susie might be able to tell me about Don's pals."

She asked if I'd like a cup of tea or coffee. I said no then decided it might be a chance to get her to talk a bit more so said yes. I stood in the hall watching her make tea in the kitchen. Tray, cups, saucers, teapot, little jug of milk.

"She was eighteen months older than me. But we were really close. Even when we were kids," she said over her shoulder. "I've got photos of her if you want." She brushed past me with the tray and set it down on a coffee table back in the living room. She went to a cupboard and brought out a large brown photo album. She showed me a photo and said it had been taken five or six years before.

Susie stood on the prom of some seaside resort on a bright summer day, staring straight into the camera. She was slim, brunette, as tall as Monica with a square-ish face and turned-up

89

nose. Her hair was tied back. She had a nice open face and a lovely smile. But there was something sad in it.

"Good-looking my sister, wasn't she? She always had blokes after her. What with that figure and her sexy lisp."

The door opened and Tracey came running in clutching a broken doll and dumped it in Monica's lap demanding she repair it.

"Later. Go out and play."

"But, Mummy!"

"In a while, sweetheart."

"What about Don?" I asked when the kid had gone.

"What about him! I've never hated anyone as much as I hated him. Not because he was a villain, though that didn't help. It was the way he treated her. Many's the time she'd come round here with lumps and bumps she'd got from a backhander. She had just such a lousy life with him."

"I can see why she'd get herself another bloke." I wondered if she knew. Of course she did. Close sisters always know. And she'd volunteered they were close. I tried to make eye contact, but she wouldn't look at me.

"Where d'you hear that from?" she finally said.

"From the bloke Don hired to follow her."

"He what! That little shit, did what!"

"Know who he was?"

She walked to the window to check on her kid. Tracey was playing hopscotch in the pavement squares. She watched her for a while then said,

"I never actually met him. She must have picked up with him maybe six months before Don died and ended a few weeks or so after the Kensington business. I've always reckoned that's what led her, to, to, you know take them pills and that … Not so much Don, although he was bad. But she had a lot of dreams and hopes about the boyfriend and a new life with him. I reckon she just couldn't handle the fallout when it ended. She once told me they'd be coming into a lot of money and they'd go off together. But it never came to anything."

"Did she say how they'd get the money?"

"No."

She let the curtain fall and went back to the sofa and poured two cups.

"Help yourself to sugar. Funnily enough she told me she'd met him because of Don."

"How d'you mean? He was a friend of Don's or something?"

"Kind of. Or a work connection or business thing. Or even to do with his underworld goings-on. I can't rightly remember now."

"You mean like maybe one of his criminal mates?"

"Kind of. What's he got to do with this? 'Cause you're the second person who's asked me about her boyfriend recently. You sure he's not important?"

"Oh, who was the first?"

"A friend of me and Susie's that turned up out of the blue asking for her. Course I told him like I told you about you know … We had a cuppa and reminisced and then just before he went he asked me if it was possible if Susie might have been seeing anyone and could he have a photo of her."

I took a sip of tea and told her I thought Susan was going to run off with the boyfriend the weekend of the raid. But Don getting killed had scuppered things.

"Susie! You're joking." She crossed her legs. Her jeans clung tightly to her thighs. She saw me looking, but it didn't seem to trouble her.

"I don't suppose there's a photo of her and the boyfriend anywhere?"

"Not that I know of."

"In the album perhaps?"

"No, this is all family stuff. If there's one of them together it'll be with Susie's gear. That'll all be up in the box room where Bobby was looking."

"Bobby?"

"Yeah, Bobby Hallet. He was the friend I was telling you about."

"Bobby Hallet?"

"Why, d'you know him?"

I wondered what Bobby had been after and what he'd found.

"Did you see what photo he took?"

"Not really; he waved one under my nose. But I didn't take all that much notice."

I asked her if he said why he wanted it. She said for old times' sake. Then I asked her if she could get the albums down for me. But it was all a bit of a palaver for her. Which I supposed meant there were too many ghosts up there. She offered to do it later after I'd gone. I gave her my card and thanked her for the tea and the chat.

"My pleasure. I'll look later. If there's anything else, I'm in most days between ten and three, that's when Tracey's at school."

"I'll remember that."

CHAPTER 21

It was a sunny afternoon with a cloudless sky but just a little bit chilly. The traffic crawled along Kilburn High Road. I bought a newspaper at the kiosk by the bridge. The smell of meat from a seedy butcher's and kebabs from a takeaway filled the air. My mobile trilled.

"It's Lisa. How you doing?"

"Okay. What's new?"

"I thought I'd touch base. I had a brainwave."

"Oh, yeah!"

"Must be catching. Working with an enquiry agent."

"So, this brainwave?"

"I went through the clothes Frank was arrested in. In case he'd managed to stuff you know what somewhere."

It was a good idea, but before she said it I knew she hadn't found anything.

"And?"

"Nothing."

"Keep thinking, about the drink, the wind, everything." Which is what I'd been doing. I knew they were important. But no lights were coming on.

My mind drifted on to Bobby as I clicked my phone off and what he'd have to say when we met. I was so busy wondering I didn't notice the Merc parked ahead. As I walked by the back door opened and Terry Norton in those small granny glasses got out.

"Got a minute?" he asked.

I looked hastily through the car window and saw George behind the wheel. I remembered his threat and looked up and down the road for a copper. But they're like buses. Never there when you need one.

"S-U-T-T-O-N," George roared. "We just wanna few words, that's all, nothing heavy."

"There might even be a few quid in it for you," Terry added, grabbing my jacket.

"Another time!" and in the absence of Camden's finest was just about to deliver a kick in the shin when George shouted,

"No one's going to hurt you if that's what you're crapping yourself about."

I was in two minds when Terry pushed me in.

"He's left his blade at home. Scout's honour."

I tumbled into the back seat. Terry slammed the door. He wouldn't be a problem if push came to shove. It was George who worried me. Nutters are unpredictable and unpredictability is dangerous. I decided to get out. Yanked the door handle to find it had a child lock. George caught my eye in the driver's mirror.

"Take it easy, Sutton, no one's going to give you any aggro." Terry got in beside his brother. "We've been following you." I hadn't noticed them, but then I hadn't been looking. I would in future. I remembered what Lisa had said that first day in her living room. 'He' meaning George 'will keep tabs on you.' I should have taken more notice.

We pulled out into the traffic, cruised up Mill Lane, and eventually turned right into Finchley Road. We sat in silence with just the purr of the engine for background sound. I was still unsure about George, but realised for the moment there was nothing I could do.

"I thought we all might have a little chat," he said, eyeing me again in the mirror. "Do each other a bit of a favour like."

"Scratch each other's back," Terry added. He pulled the sun visor down and combed his hair in its mirror, paying attention to get the mop of curls just right.

I wondered what Terry was like without George. Bobby was right. He had a lot of lip, but could he cut it on his own?

George jumped the lights at Finchley Road underground and weaved the Merc in and out of cars by Hampstead Theatre, swearing at his fellow motorists all the time.

"I thought we'd all get together," he said when he'd finished cursing. "You, me and Terry, see if we can't stop working against each other and start working together."

"Like the United Nations, you mean?"

"Don't take the piss!" Terry exclaimed. He tapped his comb on the headrest. I remembered George tapping the razor in the palm of his hand in my flat the other night and wondered what I'd said to bring this change about.

We sped down Avenue Road, past wide, elegant Edwardian houses with carriage drives and wrought-iron gates, crossed Prince Albert Road and turned into the outer circle of Regent's Park. The sun was dying in the west, its rays slanted through the trees onto the windscreen. He drove another few hundred yards and pulled over.

"Bit of class this, don't you think?" he said.

I stared at the clean, white pavements, at the overhanging trees all brown and gold, at the ornamental street lights neatly spaced at regular intervals.

"Takes dough to live in NW8, George."

"That's what I want to talk to you about. Cigar?"

"No thanks, they're bad for your health."

"Depends on your life expectancy!" A smile broke on his thick lips. A smile can light up the ugliest face, but on him it was lost.He stuck a panatella in his mouth and pushed the lighter on the dash.

"I underestimated you, Sutton."

"Oh, yeah!"

"I had a word with Leyton."

"A word!"

"A few, actually. He told me everything."

I could imagine. Poor old Ralph. First me and that headcase Brian Saxone and now the brothers grim.

"So now you know as much as me," I replied.

"You know me, Terry and Bobby were the half of the firm?"

"Yes."

"So that gives us rights to the drafts."

"But you're not getting anywhere finding them, right? Course not. Otherwise I wouldn't be getting this tour of St John's Wood." I knew there wasn't going to be any violence. Well, not today anyway. George was going to make a pitch. That's what this was all leading to. The other day he'd threatened to cut off my nose with a razor. Today it was rides around the park and free cigars.

"Me and Terry been thinking. We're going to hire you to find them drafts."

"Yeah?"

"Yeah!"

His yeah was more emphatic than mine and sitting in the back of his car with no way out persuaded me not to challenge it.

"Gonna give you a nice deal, Sutton. You find them kites. You turn them over to me for a hundred grand. On the other hand, you find them and don't turn them over, I blow your legs off."

Terry kept looking in the mirror, combing his hair.

"Good deal, ain't it, Sutton?" he said. "Better than the insurer's finder's fee. That's if they don't rook you, or keep you waiting five years for the money. And we could let you have it all in readies. 'Cause we've always got that kind of dough on hand, always, believe me, always!"

Terry wasn't wrong. Except a hundred K would always have blackmail attached to it.

"No need to think about it, Sutton. It's sorted." George exclaimed.

"Did Terry here go with you to Ralph's?" I asked.

"No. Someone had to be at the yard. Why?"

"Just wondered."

"It was just me. I can be very persuasive when I try."

"And from Ralph's you went to the B&B?"

"What's it to you!" Terry exclaimed.

George put a hand on his shoulder. Then he told me he'd turned the room upside down. Even looking in places they couldn't have possibly been. He switched the ignition off and looked around to face me.

"There's something very funny about this business, you know, Sutton."

"How d'you mean?"

"While I'm searching I'm thinking why'd he hide the drafts anyway, if he was off in the early hours." Terry stopped combing his hair. "See, I can understand sticking them under the mattress for safe keeping. But we're talking seriously hidden. Why'd he do that for three or four hours' kip? I think he was scared of something."

I didn't like George. I wouldn't give him the time of day. But you had to admire the savvy. I suppose it's what comes from being a villain.

"You're right. He was scared."

I looked out of the window for a moment. The road was empty and peaceful. The late afternoon shadows had spread across the smooth tarmac. I wondered how much to tell him and decided I had no reason to withhold this bit of the story. So I gave it to him. About Frank being attacked leaving Ralph's. His concern it wasn't coincidence. His worry over another attack during the night. George stroked his chin, his fingers rasping against his stubble.

"Scared of who? Me and Terry? We didn't know that the fucking bastard had double-crossed us at that stage. Don? Don was dead. Ralph what's-his-name? He's shit-scared of his own shadow. Who does that leave?" They turned slowly towards each other. "Bobby fucking Hallet!" George roared. "I'll fucking kill him!" He dug his thick stumpy fingers so hard into the headrest I thought they'd go through.

"Bobby doesn't have what it takes," I said.

"Well, if it's not me, or Terry here," I looked at Terry, trying to read something in his face, "or Don, then who?"

"It's the bit of the jigsaw that's missing."

The cigarette lighter popped out of the dash and George lit up and blew a plume of smoke at nice, clean Regent's Park.

"And Bobby's the piece if you ask me," he said.

"Maybe."

"If he ain't got the nouce, maybe he's teamed up with someone."

"That's more likely. The question is with who?"

He started the car. What there was left of the sun was hidden behind trees now. I sat back in the velvet upholstery trying to make sense of everything.

"If I find out Bobby's been pulling my dick, he's gonna be sorry his mother wasn't on the pill." He U-turned, the wheels screeched; I smelt rubber as he straightened up. "As to our bit of biz, Terry'll give you a mobile number to ring. You keep in touch every couple of days."

He cruised round the outer circle past a couple of joggers wearing earphones and tracksuit bottoms tucked into long white socks. We passed the mosque and the creamy white minaret beside it standing out like a gigantic ornamental candle. We turned right, through the Hanover Gate exit and up to Finchley Road. Terry handed me a slip of paper and told me not to forget to ring. I was back in Kilburn High Road inside the hour from when they'd picked me up.

"See you!" George said without turning around.

There was no goodbye from Terry. I slipped out the car and as I closed the door George took off.

CHAPTER 22

Allied Indemnity's head office was in Canary Wharf, a high-rise glass-and-steel office block with chrome outside lifts either side of the building, just to make the point they knew how to spend their investors' money. I knew Saxone would be there because I'd phoned earlier to let him know I was coming up to see him. The security officer invited me to sign in, gave me a paper visitor's badge and sent me to the ninth floor. It was all open-plan with thick brown carpeting, drop ceilings and modern zigzag fluorescent lighting.

"Mister Sutton, how do you do, I'm Zoe James, Mr Saxone's assistant." She was in her late twenties, very slim, with large blue eyes. Her black hair was swept off her face and ended in a French pleat. She wore a dark grey suit with a white blouse, and glasses, large round pink-framed glasses that complimented her complexion. "His office is just at the end of the floor." She led the way. She had a nice walk, nice legs, nice bum. Nice was a word that suited her very well. She knocked and went in. I smelt Chanel on her and it smelt — nice.

"I don't give a fuck, you bampot," Saxone was shouting down the phone. "D'you hear me? I don't give a fuck. I want this claim sorted by tomorrow. Tomorrow. And tomorrow is less than twenty-four fucking hours from now." He slammed the receiver down so hard I thought he'd break it. He pushed his chair away from his desk; it glided a foot or so and then he looked up at me.

"So, how's your day going?" I asked.

"Yes, Eddie. What can I do for you?"

"I thought I'd pop in."

"Well, now that you've popped, what d'you want?"

"Coffee, tea?" Zoe asked.

"He's not staying that long," Saxone cut in.

"Coffee thanks, no sugar."

She smiled and left.

"So, to what do I owe the pleasure?" Saxone asked as she closed the door.

"Our contract. You, me and fifteen per cent makes three! I've been waiting for it. But so far, no show. I thought I'd come and collect."

"You'll have it in the next couple of days."

"Good. Today's Monday, so it'll be with me Wednesday morning, right?"

"Anything new with the case?" he asked.

I told him about my visit from George. Which meant everybody knew about the drafts now.

"He won't find anything there. Because I went back the day after we interviewed Leyton …"

"Interviewed?"

"Oh, don't let's get into that. I looked high and low. Kamoulous told me you'd already been back there as well. So if we can't find it, he won't. Any suggestions where else we might look?"

"I'll let you know after I open my post on Wednesday."

"Ha! Ha!"

He went to the window and stared out at the BT Tower in the distance and to the east of it at the irregular lines of steel-and-glass-fronted office blocks dazzling and shimmering in the October sunshine.

"I thought sorting this out would be a piece of cake, you know."

"Well, I suppose you get easy cases as well as hard ones, luck of the draw."

His phone rang; he grabbed it up and said,

"Yes, tomorrow. T-O-M-O-R-R-O-W," he repeated sarcastically.

The door opened. Zoe returned holding a tray. Saxone's phone rang again.

"Jesus! Don't you people understand the Queen's fucking English. I do, and I'm not even English! I'll be down in two minutes. I gotta go," he said to me. "I'll be in touch," and turning to Zoe said, "One cup, and he's out of here."

She set the tray down on a small coffee table by the window. Her hair looked just slightly different, combed perhaps, and another button of her shirt was undone.

"I couldn't remember if you said black or white."

"Black, thanks. He's a real charmer, your boss."

She sat in Saxone's chair and swivelled.

"You don't want to know, but he gets results. Oh, boy! Does he get results! Which we all love because it means lots of lovely bonuses like long weekends in New York. D'you want a biscuit with that coffee?" She opened the bottom drawer of Saxone's desk and took out a tin. "Here."

"Shortcake?"

"Well, he's Scottish, isn't he? That's what they eat up there, and porridge," and she laughed.

"How long have you been working for him?"

"Well, let's see. He was investigating the Barlow House robbery in Hampstead when I joined; it was my first case. So that would be, let's see, late 2012."

"Yes, I remember that. A couple of guys hot-wired the alarm, walked in, clonked the owner and walked out with two hundred grand's worth of jewellery."

"Vincent Harris. No one to this day knows how Brian got him to divulge where the stuff was."

"Maybe he used shock tactics," I said. But the remark went over her head.

"Harris, and a guy called, called … I can't think of it."

I sipped my coffee thinking how nice it would be to undo another couple of those buttons and how pleasant what I found underneath the shirt might be. She pushed the tin across the desk and I got another whiff of Chanel.

"Naylor, no, Taylor, Don Taylor and Vincent Harris. He couldn't crack Taylor, as hard as he tried. Neither could the police for that matter. But he somehow got the truth from Harris and recovered the jewellery." She took a biscuit and broke it in half and popped a piece in her mouth. "Yes, we're all very proud of our Brian. He's got an amazing record." A crumb clung to a corner of it, then disappeared as her moist pink tongue slowly wiped her lips. "You're connected with the Weindenfeldt business, right?" I nodded. "He's really busting his chops over that one."

The phone rang. She said okay.

"I'm wanted by my lord and master. There's a crisis at Dingly Dell. That's what we call the records department. I gotta go."

"Why's he busting his chops?"

"Because he's obsessed with it to the point of taking it personally, if you ask me, which you didn't and which I therefore didn't offer an opinion about, right!"

I finished my coffee and she walked me to the lift.

"D'you ever get a call for a private investigator?" I asked.

"Now and again. If we want something checked out without our name being involved."

I gave her my card and told her I was in the book if she lost it. She smiled and said she thought there were probably quite a few things I could look forward to doing for her.

I smiled back thinking how happy I'd be to do them. Then I had this ten-second fantasy about us in her office. I take her glasses off. She pulls at a comb and her hair tumbles down. I undo the remaining buttons of the shirt and slip it off her. There's no bra and I'm not disappointed at all by what's there. They're full and round and lightly powdered with nipples big enough to get your teeth round. The nice pencil suit skirt hits the floor, as do her knickers. She kicks them and her shoes away and she's in my lap except I'm standing up! I pin her against the wall with her arms around my neck and her legs around my waist and we go at it, and at it, and at it! My heavy breathing taking in not only oxygen but the smell of Chaneled sweat that runs down her temple and between those lovely boobs. She's like a narcotic. A sweet-smelling, feline-moving, tongue-thrusting, pelvic-throbbing narcotic.

In a while I get an improved grip on her with better handfuls of that lovely arse and lay her gently across Saxone's desk. Her legs are round my waist again and I'm thrusting so hard I'm either going to give her the biggest orgasm she's ever had, or a heart attack because she has one hell of an appetite. She says 'wait' and slides from under me and drapes herself face down across the desk. She wiggles that nice pink backside, gives me a sideways glance, and as she spreads her legs beckons me with a finger.

A bell rings and the lift door opens and I'm back from Valhalla.

"Nice to meet you, Eddie! Call me. I know I'll have something for you to get your teeth into!"

"Both I and my teeth look forward to it."

CHAPTER 23

I parked in Noel Street, cut the engine and waited. The noise of Oxford Street cabs and passing buses drifted down. I gave it another minute to check I'd not been followed by George or anyone else and headed around the corner to the Poland Street car park to meet Bobby. I looked back at the entrance and, satisfied no one was following, walked up the slope. It was like most multi-storeys, large and cavernous with exaggerated noises eerily bouncing from wall to wall with the smell of petrol everywhere.I waited by the second-floor entrance looking to make sure he hadn't any friends tucked away in hiding. The odour of exhaust and sweat hung even heavier, wafted this way and that by the breeze blowing up from the staircase.

Things had happened since we'd made the appointment. There was stuff to sort out with him. I wanted to know why he'd gone to Monica's. It certainly hadn't been to renew old acquaintances. Most of all, I wanted to know what photo he'd taken from her and why. I ambled along past an elderly couple and a blonde with a tan walking to the lift. I checked some of the cars. They were empty and their bonnets and radiators hours cold.

Bobby's van was parked at the far end by itself in plenty of space. Nice for a quick getaway, I thought. I tapped on the window and motioned him to open it, but he didn't look up from the newspaper. I tapped again. I knew as I opened the door he was dead, even before I saw the wound. His body slumped towards me like a badly balanced sandbag. I grabbed it and sat him back in the driver's seat, while I had a quick shufty over my shoulder to see no one was coming.

The wound was small, just a jagged red hole with black powder burns around it. It was in his temple just by the hairline. Blood oozed from it, matting his hair. Some meandered down his jaw and neck turning his blue shirt collar purple. Some blood had hit the opposite window and streaked the glass. The wound didn't look that traumatic. I'd seen gorier sights in my shaving mirror on a bad morning. But it had been enough. No mess, no fuss. Death from a small-calibre weapon or, should I say, murder, as there was no weapon around. But now wasn't the time for post-mortems. Now was the time for a quick search and clearing off out of it. I put on a pair of latex gloves. I closed the car door and got in the passenger side. I had my hand in his jacket when he slumped forward and to my shock started a low murmuring mumble. It took me a second or two to register that he wasn't dead. I undid his collar and tried to make him comfortable. The poor sod's face was pasty white, his lips purplish blue, almost the colour of his blood-stained shirt.

"It'll be all right," I lied. "It'll be all right."

He slumped sideways so that the reflection of the wound filled the driver's mirror, reminding me what a shitty business I was in.

"I'll have an ambulance here in a jiffy."

His hand flopped onto mine.

"H,h,h,h, he made me," he croaked, his words soft and gluey and barely audible.

"Made you what, Bobby? Who?"

"Fffffforced me."

Some blood and saliva dribbled down his chin.

"Forced you to what?" I asked, putting my ear to his mouth.

"T … tttel PI was."

"Who made you?"

"Hhhhher boyfriend."

His breath felt warm on my ear. I waited for more. It would be a long wait. He'd finished, as in dead. This time for certain. I slumped back in the seat and wiped my face. "Her boyfriend," I whispered to myself. Who the hell was her boyfriend?

I went through his pockets, fags, matches, keys, some cash. I double-checked for photographs, but there weren't any. I arranged the newspaper over him so it looked like he was sleeping. Today it covered him. Tomorrow he'd probably cover it. Well, that was showbiz! I got out, took another look about, then wiped the door handles either side clean and made sure I hadn't dropped anything.

I was near the second-floor exit when a car came up the slope towards me. I shielded my face with the pretence of scratching my forehead, walked past it and down the slope to avoid anyone on the staircase or in a lift that might get stuck. I pulled my jacket collar up and kept my face covered in case there was CCTV there. At the exit, the attendant, a big black guy, twiddled the dial of a radio, too busy to even notice me strolling past him. I was glad now I hadn't brought my car in. In a half-hour's time, when the place was crawling with police, they could ask as many questions as they liked and there would be nothing to connect me.

The sun shone as I stepped onto the street. It cast a shadow across the pavement, but couldn't warm the chill inside me from hearing Bobby in my head. There was an empty phone box across the road. I thought about phoning the police then decided to do it after I'd left the area. I fumbled in my pocket for my car keys and felt the five hundred quid I'd promised Bobby. I decided on a fag and a drink before anything else.

I drove through the West End, my mind far away from the traffic. All I could see was Bobby slumped in the driver's seat, blood oozing from his temple. I still felt cold though the car heater was full on. A motor behind honked. I looked up to find I was still waiting at a green light. I passed a pub at the corner of Church Street and pulled over. I ordered a Scotch, downed it, found a pay phone in the half-empty saloon bar and dialled 999. The switching service put me through to Scotland Yard. I told them where they could find a body in a van in a multi-storey car park suffering from lead poisoning, the worst kind. The voice at the other end asked a lot of questions but got no answers then tried to stall. I gave the location again then hung up. I thought about a second Scotch, gave it a second thought and drove home.

It came up halfway through the 10 p.m. news. First, pictures of Poland Street car park, cordoned off with blue-and-white police tape and surrounded by squad cars. Then, a reporter standing outside describing how the cops had been alerted by an anonymous phone call and had found a body in a blue Escort van on the second floor. It was on the news the next morning as I shaved. The announcer said police believed it might be a gangland killing as the victim had underworld connections. The news turned to less important matters. I switched off, had breakfast and drove to Kensington nick.

CHAPTER 24

The young officer at the front desk dialled Stafford's extension, gave him my name, said yes a couple of times and asked if I'd wait in an interview room across the way. I lit up. Nerves, I suppose. The room was stark and anonymous. Just like the one at Mile Lane nick. Like they all are. Buried memories and images floated to the surface like shaken sediment. I remembered the next day after I'd beaten Joey up. I sat waiting in the same interview room where it had happened. The door opened. It was the Chief Inspector and a sergeant from CID. I stood to attention. He looked me up and down and asked if I knew why he was there.

"It's about last night's incident," he added before I could reply.

He ran over the facts, cautioned me, took my warrant card then suspended me from duty. He wanted a statement. But I declined, savvy enough to know not to say anything. It all felt a bit dreamlike as though it wasn't really happening.

"You should have known better, Sutton; what the hell did you think you were doing?" he said as I got to the door.

They all had their say. The Area Commander, with his small, white pinched face and his tunic so square on his shoulders you'd think he still had the hanger in it.

"For heaven's sake, man, and you a DC."

Sympathetic? Understanding? Not a chance! The CPS looked at it. As did the Department for Professional Standards. Then the CPS decided to prosecute. I was charged and released on police bail.

The magistrates' court was small. I looked around for familiar faces. The solicitors' well was unusually crowded. The long public benches behind the grill also full. I looked at the magistrates. I knew the middle face. I'd given evidence before it a long time ago.

108

His name was Forbes something double-barrelled. He looked me up and down over the top of bifocals, withdrew a handkerchief from his jacket sleeve and blew his nose. The Clerk of the Court beneath him drew his attention to some papers. He turned from me to him, gave him a tight little smile, then sat back against his seat one hand on top of the other.

Assault Occasioning Actual Bodily Harm, contrary to section 47 of the Offences against the Person Act 1861. People stared at me as the clerk read the charge and asked for my plea. It felt more like being in a cage than a dock. Their eyes switched to the bench. Then Joey was called, solemn but underneath loving every minute of it. Then Robins, the custody sergeant, hair greased, uniform looking almost starched. Then the two PCs. I watched Forbes something during the giving of evidence. He picked an ear, looked at the wax, then flicked it away. My brief did what he could. It lasted less than twenty minutes. Forbes something consulted his notes, consulted the clerk, then consulted his colleagues either side, then asked if I had anything further to say.

"No. Nothing, your honour."

I got six months, suspended for two years.

I knew I was out even before the hearing in front of the three of them, the Commander and the two superintendents, all sitting in a line like three monkeys. My federation brief gave it his best shot, but he might as well not have bothered. They adjourned for half an hour, then returned. I only remember the one phrase from everything said.

"You are required to resign."

Steve and a few other colleagues that dared to make contact with me wondered what I'd do, how I'd earn a living. I thought about security work. The idea lasted a day. I thought about professional debt collecting, the type without electrical toys. That idea lasted two days. In the end I decided to stick with what I knew best and got a job with a firm of enquiry agents, Hatchman and Lewis

'Honesty, Discretion, and Expertise that cannot be equalled', established in 1994 by a pair of wide boys as iffy as the people they investigated. I was with them for twelve months, then struck out on my own. And that's how it started — from a shitty back room, in an office block off Stratford Broadway in East London. Four years later I'm in a half-a-million-pound flat, earning three times as much as I would have as a DC with no one over me or any arseholes pulling my strings. I shop for my clothes in the West End and my groceries and stuff in Camden, the place for the nouveau upwardly mobile where you can buy anything from a bible to a dildo.

"Good morning!"

I looked up. Stafford stood in the doorway. He wore the same creased suit he'd worn at Frank's funeral and for all I knew the same shirt.

"How's the Weindenfeldt investigation going, Chief Inspector?" I asked.

"How can I help you? And you can put that out now. Right now!"

"Sorry!" There were no ashtrays so I gave it the old finger and thumb job. "I thought if I could help you with some information about the case, you might be able to help me in return."

"And why should I do that, Sutton? If you've got any information, you just let me have it."

"I don't suppose collaring Bobby Hallet's killer will do your record any harm."

He ran his hand over his bullet head; it seemed to glide either on grease or sweat. He opened the door and stepped into the hallway. I thought he was going to call a constable to get rid of me; instead asked someone to have his calls held.

"Now what's your game, mate?" he asked.

"No game."

"So how come you're a friend of Frank Harvey's missus?"

"I'm not. She asked me to help recover the jewellery."

"What an honest, admirable citizen!"

"All right, she'd hand it over to the insurers rather than the police, I grant you. But she's on the level, and she hates the Nortons more than you do."

"Not possible. And what about you, Mister Sutton. To what do I owe the pleasure?"

"I was hoping we might trade information. I tell you what I know about the Weindenfeldt blag and Bobby's murder. You help me with whatever you can."

He thought it over and finally said,

"You know withholding information in criminal offences is a serious matter."

"Come on, don't give me a hard time!"

"But then you'd know that, 'cause I understand you're ex-job. Ex, as in kicked out." I nodded. "What happened?" I told him. "I thought maybe you'd got the elbow for being on the take." He sat back in his chair just looking at me. He drummed his fingers on the desk. Long thin fingers that didn't go with the hangdog face and bullet head. "Okay," he said at last. "But not here. I'll give you fifteen minutes in the Highwayman, that's a pub up the road."

The saloon bar was dim and practically empty except for an old lag nursing a pint and two young lads on a fruit machine. Stafford gave them the once-over with a cold copper's stare. Speakers groaned a pop tune that swamped voices. What light there was came from square metal carriage lamps suspended from the ceiling at various points. We walked to the bar; he didn't speak which I presumed meant I was buying. I ordered two pints and carried them to a corner.

"Cheers!"

"Fifteen minutes. Start talking."

I let him have it. Well most of it. What I left out was only the important things. But then he wouldn't have known that. Nevertheless there were some tasty morsels.

"Frank Harvey planned the whole thing. It was his deal start to finish," I said.

"Tell me something I don't know."

"With Don Taylor."

"You're boring me. Tell me something I don't know."

"The rest of the firm were the Nortons and Bobby Hallet."

"Tell me something I don't know, Sutton, or it's Auf Wiedersehen."

"Frank and one of the gang planned to double-cross the other three and have it away with the gear."

"Well, well, well!" was all he said.

"It gets worse. Don's wife was having it off with someone. They somehow found out about the blag and Frank's double cross and decided to rob him of the fenced money."I wondered how they'd know.Could she and Frank have been getting it on?

"Sounds like a triple-cross, doesn't it!" he replied. Small beady eyes never left me. It was like he was trying to decide whether I was plausible before deciding whether the story was.He sat back in his seat and said, "Interesting. And where does Bobby getting done come into all of this?"

"I think Susan's boyfriend somehow latched onto Bobby thinking he could lead him to the gear and when he realised he couldn't, wasted him."

"Who's the boyfriend?"

"I don't know."

"You wouldn't be lying, would you?"

"No."

"Who was the fence?"

"I don't know," I lied.

"You don't know much, do you?"

"I try."

"Try harder." He drank some beer, some froth settled on his upper lip. He licked it away and said, "Doing up a jeweller's one thing. Not that that can be condoned," he added pointing a finger. "But blowing someone's brains out in a car park. No decent copper's going to stand for that, especially me. I thought this country was becoming too Americanised when they brought in credit cards. I'm damned if I'm going to have Chicago-styled killings in the next patch to mine." The door opened, and a couple of gents in pinstripes, carrying brollies, walked over to the bar. "Trouble is," Stafford continued, "they don't hang people any more. That's the trouble. Time was when your blinking little murderer automatically got the rope and no messing. Nowadays you do a murder,its your own cell with a shower and SKY TV. Right! Let's start again. Who's Susan's boyfriend?"

"I don't know."

"Who d'you think it might be?"

"One of the Nortons. The fence maybe. Even an enquiry agent named Lenny Warren who says he followed Susan and the boyfriend. But who knows!" Then Bobby's last words in that gluey strangled dying voice went through my mind. 'He forced me to tell who PI was' — I'd assumed he'd meant me. What if he meant Warren?

"Lenny Warren, Lenny Warren," Stafford said, taking out a pad and pencil. "I know that name. Tottenham, bit hard. I think it's got form."

I waited until he'd finished scribbling, then asked him how he'd known to collar Frank Harvey.

"You guessed it the other day at Lisa's. The gang was grassed. I got a phone call the Saturday night at the nick. She gave it to me chapter and verse."

"She?"

"She had a lisp."

"Susan Taylor."

"Right first time. I'd interviewed her earlier as soon as we knew it was Don that copped it in Kensington. I remembered the lisp. I've always had a thing about women with lisps," he said smiling for the first time. "Lisps and big tits. Never mind food being the way to a man's heart. Still, that's another story. I knew it was her straight off."

He slipped the pad and pencil in his pocket, lit a fag, said shit as he remembered he couldn't smoke in a pub any more. Then he explained how he'd organised visiting parties for the early hours. Two vehicle loads for each of the suspects. One car full of DCs and DSs and a van of plods off the patch.

"Worked like a charm," he crooned. "Bobby and his wife and George and his wife had been in their respective beds and hadn't known what hit them. Terry had just come home from clubbing it and hadn't the energy to put up any bother."

"What about Frank?" I asked.

"Like I told you. We found the pad, got the number, the rest's history."

"You lucky bastard!"

"Like they used to say; dull it's not," and he smiled again. "We split them up amongst the local nicks, Kensington, Savile Row, Paddington. I can't remember who went where offhand. But could we break them, could we hell! We had Frank on toast on account of the sawn-off we found on him matching the shell in the jeweller's ceiling. But the other three were alibied up to here," and he ran a finger across his throat. "So we had to let them go. But I knew they were the firm like I know today's Tuesday."

"Have you had the Nortons in regards Bobby's killing?"

Stafford looked up from his pint and nodded, a nod of full cynicism.

"They're like a well-rehearsed act, even in separate rooms. We'd hardly switched on the tapes before they were screaming for their briefs."

"And?"

114

"George reckons he was in the yard at the time, says he can produce a dozen witnesses. And Terry says he was out on the lorry. Their brief's Harry Draycott. D'you know him?" I shook my head. "He's done for the reputation of solicitors what the *Titanic* did for the reputation of transatlantic shipping. He had 'em out within ninety minutes."

"Reckon they might be involved?"

"They're lying about something." He took another pull on his pint. "I wouldn't fall off my chair in surprise if it turns out one or both sent Bobby to the happy hunting ground."

The pub door opened. It was beginning to fill with lunchtime trade.

"I've got a favour to ask, Chief Inspector. Could you find out who, if any, of Frank's gang ever visited him in prison?"

"Why would I want to do that?"

"Because a regular visitor might have been his partner."

"Maybe. Depends."

"On what?"

"On you coughing up more info on Bobby's death and Susan's boyfriend, and coming across with it before Halley's Comet comes around again."

He took another pull on his beer and wiped his mouth. He must have been thinking about the prison visit thing because he said,

"I underestimated you, Sutton. You're as sharp as a packet of needles, aren't you! I hope when I check you out I'm not going to find that you're a lying little shit that was kicked out for being on the take."

"Check out all you want, Stafford. I put over eighteen years of my life into the police one way and another." I was tempted to tell him about my commendation for saving a baby's life. When its coked-up mother had thrown it on a railway line and everybody had stood watching, shitting themselves that they might not get to the baby before the oncoming train got to them. Except me. Who jumped down, threw the baby to a porter on the platform and just

115

missed getting smashed to pieces in the process. Then I thought no. Let him find out himself.

A barman cleared some glasses and gave Stafford a nod of recognition. I asked Stafford if he'd been contacted by Brian Saxone.

"Saxone, Saxone? No. Who's he?"

"An investigator for the insurers."

"No."

"Unusual, isn't it? I thought they always made contact with the investigating officer."

"Not always. Because they know some investigating officers get pissed off with them earning two hundred grand a year, and poncing info off us."

"One last thing. Any chance of photos of George, Terry, in fact anyone connected to this affair?"

"I'll have them left at the desk. If I like what I learn about you." He checked his watch. "You've had your fifteen minutes, Sutton. No doubt I'll be hearing from you. Soon. If you've got any sense," and then he left, leaving me to finish my pint.

CHAPTER 25

I was in my kitchen, a modern dark grey affair with white carriage stripes. I didn't mind spending money on it, because I like cooking. I'm not cordon bleu but I can do a lot better than beans on toast. In fact, I've had my moments in the kitchen. I put the kettle on. The phone rang. It was Monica, Susan Taylor's sister, wanting to know if I'd heard the news about Bobby.

"Jesus! He was only here the other day sitting there as large as life and then I turned on the news … They said it was an underworld killing."

"Maybe."

"Poor old Bobby. What a way to go. Copped it in the side of the head, they're saying."

I asked her if she'd had a chance to look through the stuff in her box room.

"You bet I did! You don't think Bobby getting done's got anything to do with him taking the photo, do you?"

"Shouldn't think so," I said trying to sound truthful. "Any joy?"

"'Fraid not. Lots of photos of me, Susie and the family, but that's all. Thought I'd ring to let you know, what with you being so nice and understanding the other day."

I saw her in my head, the full blue shirt, the ash-blond hair, 'The best time to call's between ten and three; that's when Tracey's at school'.

"Did Bobby say why he wanted the photo?"

"Old times' sake."

Some chance, I thought. Bobby was about as sentimental as Harold Shipman.

"I remember him waving it under my nose and I said something like 'happy with that one' and he said 'yes. Just the job'. I was going to ask to have a look at it, but he put it in his pocket, then asked me how Tracey was doing. Then I forgot to ask him."

"Shame!"

"There was something that I found that maybe I should mention."

"What's that?"

"A map. Well, a sketch, I suppose you'd call it. It was all scrunched up in a ball."

"Map of what?"

"I don't know really. It's got a road marked as Queensway, an 'X' halfway along beside the number 541 and beside that the initials RL. Then a road coming off right opposite 541. It looks like Moscow Road."

I closed my eyes trying to see the sketch in my head. Then asked her if she was at home.

"Yes."

"On your own?"

"No, Bill's here."

"Good. I'm coming over."

"Bit late, isn't it? Tomorrow would be better for me," she said in a softer voice. Me too, I thought, and I knew between what times.

When I got there Bill, who was in a blue check shirt and had a beer gut hanging over brown trousers, was studying the sketch.

"This is Mister Sutton," she said.

He looked up and grunted hello. A lot of pints and no exercise later had turned the slob in the wedding photos into a bigger slob.

"Don't make no sense, do it, Mon," he said.

"Maybe Mister Sutton here can sort it."

She wore a thin grey crew-necked sweater and tight black jeans. She'd pinned her hair up. The goodies were covered, but you could tell from the nice round little arse and the impression of her nipples against the jumper what was on the menu. Bill started to hand me the piece of paper then pulled it back.

"Hang about! What's it worth?"

"How do I know until I've looked at it?"

Monica's eyes were on me. She averted them only when Bill looked at her. He offered the sketch again.

It was a pencil drawing on a shorthand pad page, as she'd described it.

"Well?" Bill asked.

"Is this Susan's handwriting?"

"No," Monica replied. "Susie's was tiny and a bit lopsided." She told me she'd found it in a plastic bag full of books and magazines and thinking there might be a photo between the pages had tipped the lot on the floor and noticed the ball of paper. "I thought it might be a receipt, so I opened it."

"And the books and stuff was definitely Susan's?"

"How many people's gear d'you think we got up there? So what's it worth?" Bill asked.

"Not a lot."

"Sure! You get it for peanuts and sell it for a few hundred."

"To who? It's a pencil diagram not a Picasso." I stuck a twenty in his shirt pocket and told him that was over the odds.

"A score! Maybe George Norton'll pay more."

"Or blow your legs off when you can't explain what it means." He thought it over and said okay.

"Atta-boy Bill!" Monica said. "Now you can give me back that fiver."

He told her to piss off. She started to say something but he fixed her with such a cold hard stare she didn't pursue it. I wondered how a couple could be so mismatched. Her, such a sweet sexy little thing, even with a squint. Him, just a slob.

119

She walked me to the door apologising for him, explaining that he got upset when he came up against things he didn't understand.

"So, what's the impotence …?" She put a hand on her lips, her other hand on my arm and smiled. "'Swhat they call a Freudian slip, isn't it? I meant, what's the importance of the sketch?"

"It means Susan and her boyfriend knew about the Kensington raid and planned to steal the fenced proceeds."

"Never," she said shaking her head. "Susie wouldn't."

"It's the only reason that fits." And whether she believed me or not, I knew it was the truth. Now all I had to do was find the boyfriend of a woman who'd briefly dated him six months ago and had herself died some weeks back, who nobody knew the identity or whereabouts of. Simple really!

CHAPTER 26

It was about 9 a.m. Lou Jackson's betting shop had not been open long. The place had been swept and vacuumed. The banks of televisions were blank. Jackson was in shirtsleeves and navy-blue trousers that looked part of a suit. They were held up with red braces that contrasted with the white shirt. He was about six foot and bald. He had a fleshy face, puffy eyelids with no lashes and thin lips that gave him a cynical countenance. He was talking to a petite black girl who stood on the business side of the counter.

"Got a minute, Mister Jackson?"

"Depends who's asking."

"Wondered if I could have a word with you about Bobby?"

"Bobby, Bobby who?"

"Come on, give me a break. Bobby Hallet."

"And you'd be? Don't tell me, a mate of his. Which I wouldn't believe if it was true."

Something told me playing it straight with Jackson was the best approach, so I did just that.

"My name's Eddie Sutton. I'm an enquiry agent. Bobby was helping me locate someone."

He took my card and looked quite impressed.

"Bobby was doing a lot of things, I'm suddenly finding out. I had the old bill in here the other day. Seems Bobby had quite a history."

"How d'you come to give him a job?"

"We needed a dogsbody, sweeping up, make tea, put the newspapers out each day. Help on the counter if necessary. I put an ad in the local rag. He sounded all right."

"Didn't you take up references?"

"Course. Turns out they came from his brother-in-law." He looked at the card again. "Enquiry agent? What's that, kind of a private detective?"

"Kind of."

He looked at me, the puffy eyelids narrowing. There was something on his mind and he was struggling with it.

"So what was Hallet helping you with?"

"Just putting me in touch with someone I needed to speak to. D'you know if he had any aggro with anyone or was being threatened?"

"Shot in the head. Can you believe it! I thought someone was pulling my leg when the cops showed up. You know, like *Candid Camera* or that geezer they used to have on the telly, what's-his-name, Beadle. You been involved in any famous cases then?"

I tapped my nose with my forefinger and said,

"Mum's the word!" I asked him again if he'd been in fights or had any aggro.

"Like I told the coppers. Only the once. Him and some geezer having a ruck one morning just as I was opening up."

"When was this?"

"About two weeks ago. Just across the road there." He pointed to the other side of the street. As I turned to look I noticed him from the corner of my eye staring hard at me. Whatever he was struggling with looked like it was bearing fruit. "Just outside the cafe they were. The bloke was prodding him in the chest and Hallet kept pushing his hand away."

"What did he look like?"

"I didn't take much notice. I only spotted him because of the car."

"Car?"

"Big, expensive, very nice."

"What make?"

"No idea," he shrugged, "a Merc, maybe."

"This geezer; was he a customer, local trader maybe?"

"Never saw him before. Haven't seen him since."

"I don't suppose you heard what they were saying?"

"What from across a busy road? Anyway, it didn't last long. He prodded Bobby, Hallet pushes him away, points a finger at him, says something, spits on the ground and walks off."

"Bobby say anything when he came to work?"

"Not him. If he said good morning that was a conversation."

The cashier came over and handed him a sheet of paper with a column of figures on it. He smiled and stuck it in his shirt pocket. I asked him if he might recognise the bloke again. But he said not.

"I don't like to stick my nose where it don't belong. Especially if there's some nutter out there with a shooter." He looked at my card again. "Mister Edward Sutton," he said, half to me, half to himself "Where have I seen you before?"

"Where d'you think?"

"You were the bloke Bobby went out the back with one afternoon for a powwow." I nodded. "You know the cops asked me to call them if I remembered anything. Or had anything new to offer. Maybe I should tell them about you." He flicked the card between his finger and thumb. "Who's to say what happened out there. I know you and Bobby had words 'cause he came back in with a face as long as a piss."

I remembered the afternoon well. Me and Bobby in the little alleyway. Me shouting at him. Lucky there hadn't been any witnesses.

"If you're going to, ring Tom Stafford at Kensington nick; he's your man."

"I might just do that. In the meantime I don't think I'll say any more to you," and without another word he turned and walked over to the cashier, and started discussing the sheet of figures she'd given him.

CHAPTER 27

I went from Lou Jackson's to Kensington nick to pick up some photos. Then went to Steve's for a game of snooker and a drink. I had the cue ball nicely lined up for the black when fingers clasped the edge of the table. I ran my eye along a hand, an arm, and found they were joined to Terry Norton.

"How you doing, Sherlock? Not putting you off, am I?"

"No. I always play with someone's hand in the way."

Terry came round the table and squinted down the cue ball, his baby face part in shadow cast by the light above the table.

"Never reckoned snooker much. My girlfriend's the one for playing with balls." He sniggered at his own joke and the sound bounced in the emptiness.

I looked at him wondering if he was capable of murder. Maybe if you're part of a crew that can steam into a jeweller's with sawn-off shotguns, perhaps you could use a handgun on your own. But for all that, he seemed to me to live in George's shadow.

"If you're wondering about the drafts. They're still missing." He said he knew. I fired the cue ball. It cracked against the black and sank it into a side pocket. "So, how can I help you?"

"Me a case of me helping you." His voice suddenly had an edge like the funnies were over and we were down to business. "Help you quite a bit as it happens." I walked around the table unable to make up my mind about the next shot. "There's been a change of plan, Eddie."

"Oh, yeah!"

"Regarding the drafts like. Instead of George getting them for a hundred grand, I get them for a hundred and twenty-five. That should make it worth your while."

I chalked the cue, and leaned across the table but my mind wasn't on the game any more.

"And where are you going to find that kind of dough, Terry?"

"We've always got money on hand. Plenty, plenty, and it's always in readies. It wouldn't be a problem for me."

"And what happens when George finds out?"

His face came out of the shadow; it looked hard with a cold stare, a look I'd not seen before. This was the younger brother in another guise. Real villain.

"I'll handle George." I wondered what handled meant but didn't ask. Not that you'd get the truth from a piece of rubbish that would turn over his own brother. "He thinks he knows everything," Terry continued, "but he don't. I play the dopey brother 'cause it suits me."

"And now it doesn't?"

"There's a lot of things George is going to find out one of these days."

"Really!"

"You better believe it." He stepped closer right into my face with a bravado I'd not expected. Then looked around to make sure he couldn't be heard. "If it hadn't been for me he'd be in clink now. 'Cause when that cab U-turned into us, they were all for getting out and legging it. And they would have if I hadn't yelled at them to lock the doors and stay put. How far d'you think four villains running down High Street Ken would have got?"

"So, you take care of George. What about the others?"

"Like who? They're nearly all dead now."

"There's Don's missus."

"Susan, Susan's dead," he said, I thought a little sadly. I wondered how he knew.

"What about Lisa Harvey?"

Terry winked and said,

"Just give her some of my dough and go on humping her, she'll be all right." He picked up a cue and feigned a shot.

125

"She's not my type, Terry."

"No? Nice little body like that."

"I'd have thought she was more George's type if she was anyone's."

"George likes 'em bunette and slim."

"Like Susan maybe?"

He stopped aiming and looked up.

"Stick to finding the drafts, Sherlock, and I'll stick to breaking cars, okay?" and he suddenly thrust the cue at me.

I had an urge to smack him in the mouth there and then but resisted. Consoled only by knowing sooner or later I'd have another Joey Farmer situation. Terry would say something once too often. Or take the piss once too often and regardless of George and his schvatze friend, that would be it.

"Everything all right, gents?" Steve asked. He stood beside me slowly wiping his hands with a tea towel, presenting Terry with two of us, one of him. Terry smiled but got the point.

"Couldn't be better, mate," he said.

"That's all right then. Wanna table?"

"Not for me, squire! Places to go. People to swindle. You know how it is! Speak to you soon, Eddie. Be lucky! And don't forget about our bit of biz." He walked down the aisle of tables to the front door and shoved it open.

"What was all that about?" Steve asked.

I told him about Susan Taylor, the sketch. The connection to the boyfriend and their attempt to rob Frank, which had made him hide the drafts so well no one can find them. And that Terry had just offered me a hundred and twenty-five K for them.

"Who d'you think the boyfriend is?"

"Someone close. That's why he's always a step ahead. He's determined to finish what he started that Saturday night with Susan, that's for sure. George, maybe Terry himself, Bobby." Then I remembered Bobby was dead. I saw him in my mind's eye

126

slumped in the van, blood meandering down his neck dripping into his shirt collar. I ran my hands through my own hair and admitted I wasn't sure what to do next.

"You humping Lisa Harvey?" Steve asked.

"Not yet."

"Then if you want some advice … walk away from it; this lunatic's already killed once. Who's to say you won't be next."

"I would, except I keep thinking of the fifty-grand reward."

My mobile trilled. It was Tom Stafford. I said hello, said I thought I must have checked out all right because his front desk had given me the photos.

"Seems you're still something of a hero at Mile Lane. I suppose any DC that puts a drug dealer in A&E can't be all bad."

"I'll take that as a compliment."

"You mentioned a face the other day, Lenny Warren? Seen him recently?"

"No. Why?"

"Someone murdered him yesterday."

My hand started shaking so much I had to make a fist to stop it. I called over to Steve for a Scotch and knocked back half in a go.

"Still there?" Stafford asked.

He let me have the details. How he'd been advised through Met co-ordination from Haringey that a cleaning lady had found him slumped in his chair with a bullet between the eyes. Whoever had done it, had then taken the office apart. All the desk drawers had been yanked out, their contents scattered. Box files tipped out. Every file in a five-drawer filing cabinet strewn over the office. A mirror smashed. Office chairs slashed and all this while Lenny was on his way to heaven. I thought maybe Steve was right. I should give it up because I was in over my head. I served summonses, tailed people. Investigating murder and mayhem wasn't in my job description. Make that murders.

"Game's changed, Eddie," Stafford was saying in my ear. "I want to know everything you know about Hallet getting done. Hackney nick tell me his place was broken into. But nothing taken even though there was a plasma TV, hi-fi, and all sorts there. First Hallet, then Warren. This headcase is after something and he's not going to stop until someone stops him."

What this headcase was after were photos of Susan's boyfriend because that was the only thing connecting Bobby and Lenny.

I couldn't tell him about Bobby's death without putting myself in the frame. But I gave him what I could which was that Susan's boyfriend connected both murders and that he was after both photos to protect his identity. And Stafford was right. He wasn't going to stop until he had them or someone stopped him. He asked again who I thought it might be? But I didn't know for sure. He asked who I thought Frank's partner had been. To that there was an answer.

"I've had an idea. Give me twenty-four hours and I think I can find out who it was."

"How?"

"You're going to have to trust me."

"Not a word I'm fond of." There was silence at the other end, which I supposed meant he was thinking it over. "Twenty-four hours. Then I want everything you've got including all the stuff you left out the other day."

"What makes you think I left stuff out?"

"Save the theatrics for when you do Hamlet. Twenty-four hours and then ex-job or not, I'll come down on you like a brick wall."

I started to say thank you, but he'd already hung up.

CHAPTER 28

I got home late afternoon. The post lay in the hall — junk mail, a final demand, a letter from Allied signed by Saxone confirming the details and percentages of our agreement, and a lilac envelope hand-addressed with what felt like keys inside. When I opened it I found it was keys to my flat and street door taped to the bottom of a lilac-coloured page that matched the envelope.

Dear Eddie

This may come as a surprise, or maybe then again not. But I've decided I want to end things between us. I used to think it was your work keeping you away from me, but I realise that was just a cover. You're your own man and just not the sort that's into commitment. I see that clearly now in your reaction to me leaving Henry. Your response, or lack of it, hurt me. Really hurt me. I expected, well, I suppose you know what I expected.

As for that night itself. The least said the better, except your work's a problem, a big problem I also don't want. But you're the biggest problem for us. I need and want something more than dating and it's just too painful hanging on for you. So I'm ending it. Take care of yourself.

Rita

Her biroed signature was faint. She'd run out of love and ink at the same time. I phoned her.

"Hello," she said her voice flat, without emotion.

"How are you?" I asked.

"Good. So there's nothing more to say, is there?"

"There's plenty. We can't just leave it like that."

"Maybe you can't. I can."

"We've got to talk."

"What about? Old times? Or about us dating for the next five years. Or maybe you want to talk about me going home that morning in a cab thinking one night you'll go out on a case and end up in the river and if the police find you, they won't even know to contact me because officially I don't exist in your life."

"Look …"

"No, you look," she exploded, "it's over. As much as it hurts me. It's over. I don't want just a casual affair, which is all you've got to offer. I've told you lots of times. I just want some happiness in my life, and that doesn't include the sweats every morning thinking today may be the last time I see you. So just get it into your thick, selfish skull, it's over," and she put the phone down on me.

I rang back, but Mandy her colleague said Rita wouldn't take the call and then in her best politest secretarial college-trained voice suggested I didn't call again, or Rita's mobile, and then she put the phone down on me as well.

I sat in my office. The day was grey anyway, which made everything seem even gloomier. I turned on the lights and for no reason at all got the strangest feeling something was wrong. Not that there was anything out of place. The papers on my office desk were as left, as were the files in the filing cabinet. I went into the kitchen, everything including unwashed dishes from the night before were as left. Everything in the fridge including a .38 wrapped in foil in a cheese box was okay. Years ago I'd left the keys of a flat I was selling with an estate agent so they could show people around in my absence, and though nothing was ever moved, I somehow always knew when they'd been there. It was like that now. But this flat wasn't in the hands of any agent.

The phone rang startling me. It rang twice more before I answered it. I hoped it was Rita. It was Lisa.

"Eddie. How are you? You okay? You sound funny."

"I'm fine. What's up?"

"Well, I hope this isn't gonna to sound cockeyed but …" I sat back in my chair and looked about the office. There was nothing out of place. Even the Pirelli calendar with the blonde in nothing but a fur G-string to protect her against October and the onset of autumn was straight. But I had the strangest feeling. "The thing is," she continued, "I've been rereading my Franky's letter yet again, and trying to think like Frank."

"And?"

"Don't they call vodka and orange a screwdriver?"

"Yeah, I think they do."

"So?"

"So, what?"

"Don't you see? Room twelve and screwdrivers."

"You mean he's hidden the drafts somewhere in the room that needs a screwdriver to get at them?"

"Exactly!" I was about to tell her that it sounded a bit far-fetched when she said, "If it's not connected, then why'd he go to the trouble of spinning a fairy tale about holidays we ain't had and drinks I don't drink?" There was silence and then she asked me again what I thought, which was that it sounded a bit far-fetched. "There's something else, Eddie."

"Go on."

"A wind that's spent. I've given that some thought as well."

"And?"

"It's a draft. A wind that's spent is a draft, though you spell it different."

"Okay. I'll meet you there in a half an hour. But, Lisa …"

"Yeah?"

"Don't raise your hopes too high."

131

"One other thing before I go, Eddie. I had Stafford round again. He wanted to know if I was close to Susan Taylor."

"Were you?"

"I hardly knew her. But he kept on about did Frank know her and did he or anyone ever mention she might be seeing someone on the side and if so who it might be."

"Did Frank know her?"

"She was Don's wife. They're bound to have met."

"I suppose so" I replied.

"He wanted to know if anyone had ever dropped a name or knew what line of work the boyfriend might have been in. Not that I'd tell him even if I knew." I was listening to her but kept looking around the office trying to understand what was chafing me. "He's usually such a cocky little bastard," Lisa went on, "but not this time. Anyway, see you in a bit!"

I hung up thinking it was pretty cute of her connecting the drink with the screwdriver and the wind to a draft. So far she'd struck me as just a looker with a body. Suddenly I was seeing something else as well. I found two screwdrivers and as I turned out the lights, looked around the office again,finally realising what had been wrong. I'd closed the office door before leaving this morning and come back to find it ajar. Someone had been in here while I'd been out.

CHAPTER 29

She was already there waiting in her car. She smiled and said hello. She wore black trousers and a black heavy wrap-around cardigan. The wind lifted its floppy collar so that it momentarily framed her short blond hair. We stepped into the warm reception area of the hotel. Kamoulous was sitting behind a desk sorting out some keys. His five o'clock shadow right on time. He looked up, smiled at Lisa. Saw me and stopped smiling.

"Remember me? Of course you do."

"What you want?"

"Key to room twelve, please."

"Take a walk, mister!"

"No key. No money."

"They give you the money from the TV?"

"Sure."

"Liar! They never heard of you. I phoned them."

"That's because I'm with Sky now."

"Sure, sure, you can still take a walk." I drew ten fivers and held them in front of him. He looked at me like he was doing me a whole favour taking them and handed over the key. "The room's booked out for someone for 5.30 p.m." He looked at his watch. "You got thirty minutes. Then you're out. O-U-T."

I locked the door and looked around the room. All the comings and goings, me, Saxone, George, hadn't changed it. It was still a cheap and nasty flop. She took off her cardigan and threw it on the bed. Then rolled up the sleeves of a denim shirt.

"I'm going to unscrew anything that's unscrewable."

I looked from the wall mirror, to the shaver point, to the door handle plate, to the wash-hand basin, realising how many possibilities there were.

"Okay, Lisa. But we do it systematically, we'll go round clockwise and unscrew whatever we can. If there's nothing there, we replace it before going on to the next thing. Clear?"

"As a bell." She came over and pecked me on the cheek. "I really appreciate this, Eddie."

The first thing was the large square mirror above the washbasin. I undid the screws while she eased the mirror away from the wall. We both peered behind it. Nothing, except a dirty brown watermark on the paper. She unscrewed the shaver point beside it, her red varnished fingernails picked the screw from the socket then pulled the plastic unit away from the wall. The cavity behind it was filled with nothing but a tangle of wires. There was nothing either in the hollow of the towel rail beside it. She looked over my way as I replaced it and said,

"So far not so good. Never mind, early days."

We stripped the bed for good measure. I opened the wardrobe and searched inside it, then above it, and beneath it. She unscrewed the door handle fitting. I watched her, her wet pink tongue clamped between her teeth as she carefully undid the screws. She pulled the plate and the door handle away, but there was nothing more exciting than varnish stains. I undid the light switch and on impulse stood on a chair and undid the light rose.

The grey afternoon was turning slaty dusk. Kamoulous had said thirty minutes. Our time was nearly up.

"Where the hell are they!" she suddenly shouted, throwing the blankets back across the bed.

Someone tried the door then knocked. I looked around the room; everything was as we'd found it. I opened up. Kamoulous walked in.

"You find anything here?"

"What's there to find?" I replied.

"You won't find nothing here. Na! Not here. The police pulled this place apart. They had dogs here, equipment, men, everything. But I said that to you already. If they found something they'd have said. Unless they stuck to it themselves."

"What can I do for you?"

"Time's up. My five-thirty people's arrived."

Lisa was putting some lipstick on in the mirror when Saxone appeared behind Kamoulous and shoved him across the room.

"Time's up when we say it is." Kamoulous half-stumbled, half-sprawled like a runner breasting a finishing tape. He tried to find his balance but couldn't and landed on the floor in the corner of the room. He just sat there open-mouthed, startled by the suddenness of what had happened, rubbing his elbow. "Time's up when we say it is," Saxone repeated.

"Where the hell did you spring from?" I asked.

"I was in the area. I thought I'd nose around."

"Just like that!"

"Why not? It's a free country. Find anything?"

"No."

"Sure?"

"Would I lie to you?"

"What are ...?"

"Shut it!" Saxone snapped at Kamoulous. He pulled the blankets clear of the bed.

"You didn't answer my question. How come you're here?"

"I'm after the same thing as you. It's in my interest to find it first." He checked a wallpaper join and then, as though he'd only just noticed her, though he knew full well she was there, bid Lisa good afternoon.

"Maybe if we're done here, Eddie, we should go."

Saxone smiled at her, then grabbed her shoulder bag and before either of us could do anything, tipped everything out so that make-up, comb, purse, keys spilled onto the floor. A small perfume spray bounced on the carpet and came to rest by his shoe. He picked it up along with the other items and put them back in the bag.

"Well, at least we know you don't have any banker's drafts tucked away, lassie."

She fixed him with such a cold hard stare of hatred it made me think she might be capable of murder.

"If my Frank was alive," she hissed.

"But he's not, is he!"

I wondered what had brought Saxone here just at that moment. The man had a knack of always being in the right place at the right time. And an answer popped into my head.

"They're well hidden, wherever they are," he said. He buttoned his jacket and preened himself in the wash-hand basin mirror, pulling at shags of his blond hair then straightening his maroon silk tie knot. He moved closer to the mirror and inspected his teeth, small white even little choppers that'd bite your ear off in a fight. "Wouldn't you say, Eddie?", his Scottish accent grating on me.

"I'll let you know if I find them."

He pulled open the wardrobe door and looked inside. He ran his hand along its inside, then standing on a chair, ran a hand along its top. I put on my jacket and motioned Lisa towards the door.

"See you, Saxone."

"Hey, laddie, you've forgotten something." He picked a screwdriver off the bed and slipped it into the top pocket of my jacket so that it stuck out like a small aerial. He looked at Lisa, then back at me and said, "You just never know when you're going to come across something that needs a good screwing, do you!"

I walked Lisa back to her car. She rested her bag on its roof and rummaged for her keys.

"D'you think we should have left that scumbag up there? Suppose he finds something?"

"He won't. He's as confused as us."

A hint of a smile edged at the corner of her mouth.

"Sorry about dragging you over here. I was certain the drink and the screwdriver and the drafts were connected."

I told her she'd done well making the connections. I thought again how bright that actually was. She was right. They were tied. The problem was we just couldn't see how. She found the keys and unlocked her car.

"Mind if I borrow Frank's letter?"

She looked in her pocket.

"You won't lose it, will you. It's special even though I haven't a clue what it's about."

"I won't lose it."

She got in her car, stole a quick look at herself in the mirror and drove off, while I sat in mine, closed my eyes and tried to think where the hell else in that room Frank could have hidden those two damn bits of paper.

CHAPTER 30

I went back to Queensway the next morning. He was standing with his back to me, slightly stooped over a counter, his thinning grey hair hanging over his starched white collar. He turned around, saw me and clutching a hand to his chest almost jumped backwards.

"What d'you want?" he demanded and turned from me to look for Saxone.

His shop was large, almost cavernous, with a polished floor. The counters, wood and glass, were old-fashioned but the stuff inside them was modern and expensive.

"What d'you want?" he asked again, starting to move away. "I told your friend everything."

A film of sweat broke on his upper lip. He wiped it away with the palm of his hand. I grabbed him by his shirt and pulled him towards me.

"You wouldn't want my friend to come back and give you another going over, would you?"

"I told you everything."

"My friend's a lunatic."

"I'm still getting over the other night, you know that. My doctor thinks I had an attack of nerves. Here, look!" He pulled a little bottle of tablets from his waistcoat pocket and waved it under my nose. "Valium for my nerves," he spat. "I should have told him what happened."

"Yeah, right! Cue the violins. I've got some photos I want you to look at. Just tell me if you recognise anyone." He looked at me quizzically and asked if that was all. Then looked again to reassure himself Saxone wasn't there. "And no lies, right!"

138

A tall girl in a black raincoat and beret peered at the jewellery and antiques in the window, started to come in then changed her mind. I handed Leyton the first photo. He put on a pair of black horn-rimmed specs and looked at it.

"What's this, a joke?" he asked. "You trying to trick me? That's Frank Harvey." I handed him the second photo. "And that's his wife, I think her name's Lisa. I met her a couple of times."

The third photo was of Susan Taylor. I watched him. He said he didn't know her. I asked him if he was sure. He still said no.The next was a photo of Bobby Hallet. He didn't know him either. I studied his face. When I was certain he wasn't lying, I handed him another, which was of George Norton.

"This one!" he cursed. "This animal was here the other day. He threatened to put me in a car crusher. This animal's as bad as your friend." Worse, I was about to say, when he added, "So I told him about the drafts."

"Ever see him before the other day?"

"No. And if I never see him again it'll be too soon."

The next photo was of Don. He looked at it started to shake his head, then looked at it again and handed it back.

"Well?

"No. Only Frank, Lisa, and the animal." And then I handed him a photo of Terry; I waited. He studied it. I studied him. But there wasn't a flicker of recognition and when he said no I believed him. "Let me have a look at the other one again."

"Which?"

"The one before last." Leyton looked at it. Perused Don's thin, swarthy face, his thick eyebrows, the narrow ski-slope shape of a nose, his hair full at the sides with long sideburns, almost a 1970s-style haircut. "This one!" he said.

"What about him?"

"He was the one that came with Frank to do the business before the robbery."

139

"You sure?"

"Yes."

"What's his name?" But Leyton couldn't tell me. I asked him three times, even threatened him with the same treatment Saxone had given him. But he just didn't know.

"Honest, honest," he kept repeating, his Adam's apple rising and falling into the knot of his paisley pattern bow tie. "I don't know. Frank just introduced him as his partner."

I lit a ciggie without offering and took a drag. So it had been Frank and Don. It explained for certain how Susan had known where and when the gear would be fenced. Because she'd got it from Don, and how her boyfriend had known where to wait. I collected the photos.

"Who is he?" Leyton asked.

"Who?"

"The man in the photo?"

"What photo?" He started to say something, but the shop door opened and the window-shopper came in and I left.

CHAPTER 31

I rang Monica and said I wanted to look at everything Susan had left. She suggested 10.30 a.m. She smiled and said how nice it was to see me. Then apologised again for her husband's behaviour the other evening. She wore green leggings and a tight fitting yellow shirt. She led me into the lounge where slivers of sunlight streamed through the windows and fell across the room. She turned down the hi-fi to a whisper.

"That's better," she said. "There's really not much up there apart from the sketch."

"I'd like to have a look anyway."

"Sure. Now?"

"If you can spare the time?"

"I'm all yours. I don't pick Tracey up until three," and moved past me closer than was necessary. "Follow me."

She stood on the first stair, so she was at my height, eye to eye.

"If there's anything you fancy when you're up there, Eddie, just help yourself."

We turfed the contents of the bag onto the floor. There were magazines, family photos, a compact bag, CDs, Michael Jackson and Sting. Monica was on her knees opposite me, her legs tucked underneath her so that the leggings were pulled tight across her thighs and over her flat stomach. She leaned over examining the contents, then looked up to find me looking at her.

"Anything of interest?"

"You could say that." I pulled her towards me and kissed her.

"You didn't really come here to see Susie's stuff, did you? Did you?" she demanded.

"Not really!" I kissed her again.

141

She pressed herself tightly to me and began kissing me as I carried her into her bedroom.

She lay back on the bed, blond hair on a green duvet. I undid her shirt. She had firm white breasts with hardened nipples. She reached out and unbuttoned my shirt. Kissed my chest then ran her fingernails down my body, then undid my belt and fly zip.

"D'you have anything with you?"

"I've got a rabbit's foot on my key ring."

"Very funny!" She pushed me away playfully. "You're a waste of time, Eddie Sutton."

"You reckon?"

"Well, on second thoughts. Maybe not," she said as she rolled on top of me.

I pulled down her knickers. I gazed at her thighs and the crop of mousy pubic hair between them. She twisted over the edge of the bed searching in a bedside drawer. Her lovely little arse like a pink peach wriggling in front of me. By the time she'd turned around I was out of my jeans and boxer shorts.

"Here take …" She stopped mid-sentence and copping a look at the goods said, "Jesus! You must have been right at the front of the queue."

I felt myself getting harder and harder. She stretched back, her arms across the pillow and suddenly, quite breathlessly said,

"Show me what you can do with it, Eddie!"

I slid inside her easily because she was so wet. She put her arms around my neck, pulling me closer, she arched herself accommodating me deeper and deeper into her. The only sounds from her were ooohs and aaahs ripping into my ears, their visual interpretation written in the pleasure on her face. She closed her eyes and breathed heavily as if the pleasure could be inhaled as well.

The determined thrusting and response created a rhythm, and we went hard at it. Synchronised, violently, unremitting. Her ooohing and aaahing becoming louder and louder and then,

"Don't stop, Eddie. Don't stop! It's been so long since I was given a good seeing-to. I just want you to fuck the living daylights out of me!"

And I did. On and on taking her higher and higher. I came. She came. I expected her to be a shrieker. But she just turned away and convulsed with some kind of skeletal tremor that shook her throughout until she was spent. And then she lay there, sprawled, eyes closed, with a huge grin on her face.

"You all right?" I asked.

"Oh, yeah! I'm very all right. You can come and investigate me any time you like!"

She looked so horny laying there, her hair a mess, her body sweating from the sex. I was thinking of turning her onto her knees and forearms and giving an encore when she pulled the duvet to her chin and said,

"Life's funny, isn't it!"

"How d'you mean?"

"Well, there's me always cursing Don. Yet if it hadn't been for him, I wouldn't have met you."

She moved nearer, her warmth and the smell of her perfume and sweat from all that thrashing and rocking around rekindling the lust in me.

"Talking of Don," I said. "I heard a whisper about him the other day. Did you know he did the Barlow House job in Hampstead?"

"Yeah, with Vinny Harris. Everyone knows that."

"What happened?"

She pressed herself closer.

"What do I get as a reward for telling?"

"Funny you should mention that!"

She took me in her hands and started kneading me gently.

"Hmmm, that'll do nicely." I pulled her towards me and kissed her. "You should be made to have to have a licence for this thing, Eddie."

"So what happened?"

"Later."

"No. Now."

"Hmmm!" she exclaimed testily. "You pick your moments, don't you? Vinny was a builder. Quite a big bloke. But I'll bet not as big as you," she whispered coquettishly. I smiled. She smiled too, enjoying her own sauciness, being with a man, and the pillow banter that went with it.

She told me how Don had plotted the job and he and Vinny did it. They'd copped about ten grand in cash and over two hundred grand in jewellery. They'd split the money and stashed the gems in a safety-deposit box Vinny owned, waiting for the heat to lift. The police had fancied Don for it straight off but couldn't prove anything.

"The next thing you know," she continued, "the insurance people have got their hands on Vinnie and he gives up the gear."

"You mean the old bill?"

"No. The insurers."

"How come?"

"The rumour was they were grassed, and by someone close to them 'cause there could only have been three or four people that knew about them doing the job. They're lucky they didn't end up inside!"

She ran her hand slowly over my forehead, tracing the line of my eyebrows with a finger.

"You're a real little rascal, aren't you, d'you know that! Is there a Mrs Investigator?"

"No."

"Really! How'd someone like you slip through a woman's hands?"

"I'm far too young to get married!"

"Talking of slipping through a woman's hands …"

I put mine on hers.

"How come neither Don or Vinnie were prosecuted?"

"Something about, what do they call them? The CSP or such like."

"You mean the CPS?"

"Yeah. Not happy about the way a confession was got or the gear recovered. At least, that's what I heard. You sure you're not married, Eddie?"

"I think I'd have remembered, toots! How d'you hear all this?"

She hesitated for a moment and said,

"Susie used to tell me stuff."

"Some story!"

"I've got a much better story I can tell you, Eddie. Once upon a time," she said very softly, her breath filling my ear, "there was this girl who was owed a reward from this dishy bloke. But this guy wouldn't stop talking so she had to sit astride him to get his attention. Are you familiar with this yarn, Eddie?"

"Yeah, and I think I know how it ends."

"Good. Very good. You must read the same books as me."

"Well, we're definitely on the same page here. That's for sure."

She slid on top of me, then leaned back and closed her eyes. She began slowly gyrating herself on me gathering herself into a gradual frenzy. She had a nice face, great boobs, was good in bed and I thought what a nice regular situation this could become. She took my head between her hands and started kissing me. Then put my face right into those lovely tits, rocking back and forth, back and forth. This time she did shriek, with 'yes, yes, yes, yes' until she nearly deafened me. And then in a raking, gasping, panting breath there came one final, gigantic, shrieking 'YES!'

I'd dozed and came to with a start.

"Eddie, wake up!" The afternoon had greyed.

"What's the matter?" I asked. She was out of the bed gathering up her clothes. "What's the matter?"

"It's nearly three. I have to pick Tracey up. We've got to get dressed."

"It won't matter if you're a few minutes late."

"Yes, it will." She put on her knickers, her shirt, flicked her hair over the collar then pulled on her leggings. She came into my arms soft and warm and smelling of sex. "You're something else, Eddie. D'you know that! Really, something else!"

"Speak to you soon."

"Make it real soon. Because I think you'd like my party piece," she said, squeezing herself against me.

"And what's that?"

"Giving this monster," she said, sliding her hand across my flies, "a really good sucking and staying down on it until you're ready to fill me up with him!"

"Real soon. You can rely on it!"

CHAPTER 32

I felt very comfy on my sofa with my feet up on the coffee table and a glass of Jack Daniels in my hand. In the corner of the living room a fat American police chief sat in an oak-panelled courtroom giving evidence to spellbound jurors. The phone rang. It was a different police chief.

"Eddie? Tom Stafford."

"I was just about to ring you."

"Well, there's a coincidence," he said sarcastically. "So? What's the news from Camden Town?"

I took another swig and put the drink down.

"Frank Harvey's partner was Don Taylor."

"How d'you know?"

"It doesn't matter. But it's legit. My guess is Don told Susan about the blag, and the proposed double-cross. She's already involved with her boyfriend and they decide on a little free, help yourself, enterprise."

"So, who's the boyfriend?"

"I think Terry Norton. But how you'll prove it, is another matter."

"I had the Nortons in again this afternoon."

"And?"

"I've had more conversation from people on life-support machines."

The chief of police on the screen was now in deep discussion with the DA. But I was too concerned with my own puzzles.

"What else, Eddie?"

"The jewellery was fenced for a million quid. That's what Harvey had at the B&B, not the jewellery."

He gave a long low whistle, then said,

"A million! That takes some schlepping around." I wondered whether to tell him it was in drafts and decided not to. "Well, I've got some news for you," Stafford said. "I've got a lead on Bobby's murder. But the person's description doesn't fit with Terry." He began to tell me that a young lad at the car park, who washed cars for account customers, had been on the second floor getting a hose from a cupboard and thought he'd seen someone by Bobby's van. "He reckoned about six foot, late thirties, early forties, dark hair." I felt a cold shiver go right through me and end in nausea in my stomach. "Still there, Eddie?" he asked. "Says he saw the bloke, tapping on Bobby's window. He didn't take much notice at the time because he was in a hurry."

I put my hand over the receiver, took a deep breath and closed my eyes.

"Can he make an ID?" I asked.

"Bit iffy. Reckons he saw the geezer on the next level down a few minutes later. But he was scratching his head so his face was obscured."

"Shame."

"But get this. Thinks the bloke was wearing latex gloves."

My mind went back to the car park. I remembered the smells and the litter being blown around, me checking cars to make sure Bobby hadn't friends in hiding. There hadn't been more than fifteen or twenty cars, practically empty. How come I hadn't noticed the boy? But then I'd been busy once I'd opened the van door. Still, I should have removed my gloves sooner. I asked if there was CCTV. But I knew there wasn't or else we wouldn't be having this tête-à-tête.

"Cameras all over the place. Some working, some not. But the three on that floor were all smashed."

It meant now even if I was allowed, I couldn't go back there to check details that might help me find Bobby's killer.

" We've had the post-mortem results on Bobby," he continued.

"Oh, yes!"

"Bullet from a 9 mm Smith and Wesson. Entered the left temporal region close range. It passed through the brain and lodged in the right parietal lobe. In other words, he copped one in the head straight off. They reckon death would have been instantaneous."

I could have told him that it wasn't. That Bobby had struggled to stay alive. That he'd fought for breath and gurgled and burbled to tell me something I couldn't understand.

"We're still waiting for Lenny's."

"Pound to a penny, you'll find the same gun did it."

"Which reminds me. Might need your fingerprints."

"Why?"

"SOCO's still at Lenny's. We'll need yours, to eliminate you from our enquiries. They're trying to finish up as quickly as possible. Not that it matters. Because Lenny won't be conducting business from there any more. Or anywhere else for that matter."

Indeed he wouldn't and it gave me an idea. I thanked Stafford for his call and told him he could ring me for whenever he needed my dabs.

CHAPTER 33

The fact that poor Lenny wouldn't be doing anything again persuaded me to take a chance and see if I could blag my way into Swinburn's, the security storage firm where Lenny's papers were archived. I typed up a supposed letter of authority from him giving me permission to collect his files. It's not that they could have checked its authenticity with him because Lenny was lying in a morgue. However, with all this data protection shit these days I knew the chances were slim. So plan B was to take five hundred quid in readies with me to see if anyone there was up for just letting me cop a look through his 2012 and 2013 stuff.

My satnav said straight on. 1309 Upper Street was halfway between Canonbury and the Angel. I kerb-crawled checking numbers. I passed a pizza takeaway, an insurance broker and a firm of solicitors, all the businesses nicely numbered, nicely signed. A car behind hooted at my ten miles an hour but I took no notice. I passed another firm of solicitors, the sun reflecting on their brass plate screwed to crumbling brickwork. The road swept in a bend. I continued checking numbers. 1271, 1273, 1275, restaurants, estate agents, door after door, all fortunately numbered. The professional people, accountants, dentists, all with nice brass plates. Swinburn's was just ahead. It too was well signed with a large metal plate above its front door. Looking at it, and the shops and the signs and the doors, a thought suddenly tumbled into my head. It was so clear I couldn't understand why I hadn't thought of it before. The notion took hold so strongly a vein in my temple started throbbing uncontrollably and the palms of my hands began sweating so much they nearly slipped off the steering wheel. 'That was it. That had to be it,' I found myself saying over and over. It was all so bloody obvious. Once it was obvious! And yet we'd all missed it. Me, Lisa, Saxone, George. Just the way Frank knew we would. It took a Frank Harvey to think of a hiding place like that. A place so apparent we'd all miss it. That's why he'd sent his wife the crazy letter he had.

I U-turned violently deciding to go back to the Parkland instead of Swinburn's. But via my place to pick up my .38, just in case! I took the stairs two at a time, pulled my mobile and rang Lisa.

"I've sussed it!" I exclaimed.

"What d'you mean?"

"I know where the banker's drafts are."

"Where?" she asked her voice excited and demanding.

I wanted to tell her but the copper in me dictated caution.

"Meet me at the Parkland as soon as you can."

"Where's the money, Eddie?"

"The Parkland as soon as you can."

My next call was to Stafford. A voice at the other end said he was in conference.

"Don't piss me around. Get him. Tell him it's Eddie Sutton, and I've found the money." I was speaking to Stafford in less than half a minute. He too wanted to know where the money was.

"First, go to a firm called Swinburn's, 1309 Upper Street in Islington. You want any photos they've got with Lenny Warren's stuff from around 2012 and 2013."

"Just like that!"

"Yes. Tell them it's connected with a murder enquiry. And if they give you any data protection crap, stick your ID down their throats. Tell them Lenny won't be making any complaints on account of him having had his brains blown out. And if that's not enough, tell them you'll have Health and Safety, the local nick and anyone else you can think of on their case until they'd wished they'd never heard of you."

"What's so special about the photos?"

"If there are any, they'll identify Bobby and Lenny's killer."

"If this is a stroke, Eddie, you are going to be seriously sorry."

"It's no stroke. I can't guarantee there's a photo. But if there is one, it'll do what I just said."

"1309, you say. I'll be there tout-suite." He paused for a long moment, I suppose, while he wrote the address down. "What about the money? The desk said you've found it."

"I think so. Meet me at the Parkland afterwards."

He sighed a deep sigh. I wasn't sure if it was resignation or him just trying to hang onto his temper.

"I'm on my way."

I hung up and I too was on my way.

CHAPTER 34

Lisa was just parking when I got there. The first thing she said was, "Where's the money?" Then remembered her manners, smiled said hello, then asked again where the money was.

"Come, I'll show you." I pushed open the hotel door and ushered her ahead of me.

The small reception area was empty as was Kamoulous's alcove, but we could hear him in the back humming 'Smoke Gets In Your Eyes'. I headed for the stairs, Lisa pointed to the key rack and said,

"You'll need the key."

"No."

Everyone had used the key. They'd stormed into room twelve and turned it upside down. We too had fallen for the obvious. But the best place to hide something from someone was right under their nose. I opened the fire door on the first-floor landing, Lisa behind me breathless with excitement. The long carpeted corridor empty and silent. It closed with a soft hush that complimented the silence around us. I walked slowly past each numbered door remembering how I'd passed each numbered shop in Upper Street. We stopped at room twelve. Lisa stood there looking quizzically at me.

"When's a dish that's a dish, not a dish?"

"What!"

"And then you threw your vodka and orange at the door," I said paraphrasing his letter. I could see she still didn't get it. "You were right, Lisa. The vodka and orange was about a screwdriver." I tapped the room number attached to the door. "The dish is a plate. My guess is the drafts are behind here."

"Jesus Christ!" she exclaimed and came closer to peer over my shoulder, so close we were touching. I could feel her breasts pressing against me and the warmth of her body as she became more and more excited.

The screws came out easily. I half-edged the plate away from the door, and there behind it were two neatly folded pieces of paper. I could feel a smile breaking on me. I opened them out. They were two banker's drafts made on the Banque Nationale de Belgique. They were just like cheques in a mauvish-green colour with the bank's logo of a star stencilled in white in the centre and their head office address printed in black across the top. One made out to Frank, the other to Don Taylor. That's why Frank had had both. Because Don was dead. He was in for a million quid because there was no one to share it with. I looked at them again. They didn't look anything out of the ordinary and yet they'd caused so much aggro. Lisa took them from me and stared at them for a long time, then clutched them to her breasts.

"Fifty thousand quid! Eddie, Eddie, I can't believe it!" she squealed again then screwed her face in a childlike grin and kissed both pieces of paper. "Fifty thousand quid! I just cannot believe it." She threw her arms around my neck and planted a great big kiss on my cheek. "You clever, clever bugger. Jeff said you was the best and he was right. But what made you look there? Oh, I could bite lumps out of you. You're brilliant."

I'd be even more so, when she got seventy-five.

"I was in Upper Street checking door number plates for an address and it suddenly clicked. Frank's letter, room twelve, everything."

She stared at the drafts again.

"So what happens next?"

What happened next was that the fire door at the end of the corridor opened. I tried hurriedly to re-screw the number plate, but my haste made me all fingers and thumbs. Before the thing was properly back in place Brian Saxone was standing in front of me. He said nothing. He just stood there taking in the scene, me, screwdriver in hand, the door number plate hanging lopsided on the door by a screw.

"I came up here for another search," he said, showing me the room key. "Seems I'm too late."

"That's showbiz!" I replied.

"Behind the sodding door plate. Shit! What made you look there?"

I was about to tell him when he snatched the drafts from Lisa's hand. But as he started to read them, I snatched them out of his and put them in my trouser pocket.

"You can look all you want after I get a receipt."

"You know they're Allied's property, don't you?"

"Wouldn't deny it. We're not laying claim to them, only the finder's reward."

"We?"

"Me. Mrs Harvey here is just moral support."

Lisa started to say something, tumbled what I was on about and closed her mouth.

"May I?"

"Receipt first."

"Sounds like you don't trust me."

"Of course I do. Receipt first."

He reached inside his pocket. The hair on my neck rose as his hand came slowly out of his jacket. I braced myself.

"It's an Allied Indemnity scratch pad, with address and logo on it," he said, waving it under my nose.

I took a deep breath and relaxed. He started writing, but I insisted on dictating the contents. I made it long and windy. About him being an employee representing the insurance company acknowledging me as having found the drafts and that I was handing them over to him on the basis of the agreed reward for so doing. It went on a bit, me bunging everything I could hastily think of to prevent those polished little bastards in Canary Wharf reneging on the deal.

"You wouldn't like this signed in blood, would you, laddie!" he said at last.

I read the receipt — twice, handed it back to him and told him to sign it then print his name alongside his position with the company. Then I handed him the drafts.

"Behind the door number plate!" he sighed looking at them.

"How long before Mister Sutton gets his dough?" Lisa asked.

"Month, six weeks perhaps."

"Don't rush yourself, will you!"

"These things take time." He held the drafts up to the light. "Hmm, behind the bloody door plate! I should have guessed it would be somewhere like that. Oh well!" He put them in his pocket. "I'll be in touch."

"If you're not, I will be," I replied.

CHAPTER 35

Lisa and I sat in the foyer with its sad decorations and badly upholstered armchairs. Kamoulous asked us what we were waiting for and when I told him the police, he became nervous. He made us each a cup of tea for three quid, then stepped into his reception alcove and started whistling 'Smoke Gets In Your Eyes' again. He got through a couple of bars, looked over his shoulder and said,

"What's the law want with this place? I told you they been over here with a fine-tooth brush."

"Comb," Lisa said.

"What?"

"It doesn't matter."

"What about you two? You was here only a couple of days back."

"Double-checking."

"And the Scotchman?"

"Also double-checking."

"Seems like a lot of double-checking going on. I don't like this place being so popular. It's bad for business. How long they gonna be?"

I told him not long. He hung some keys on a peg and went back to whistling. The front door opened and an elderly woman with a plastic shopping bag came in, and went upstairs. Lisa took a sip of tea and said,

"Why's the law really coming here?"

"I promised to tell Stafford where the drafts were. He's also hopefully got some photos I want."

" Any reason for me to stay?"

"No."

"Then I'm off. What happens about the drafts?"

"I'll ring Saxone in the morning, remind him to pull his finger out."

"Good!" She moved closer and playfully jabbed her finger at my shoulder. "You were brilliant at finding them drafts, d'you know that, absolutely brilliant." I shrugged unable to think of anything to say. "We'll have to get together for a celebratory drink on me," she added, gave me another peck on the cheek and left.

Kamoulous had moved on to 'Greensleeves'. I lit a cigarette; I'd noticed he smoked on the premises so he was hardly going to complain about me. A picture of Frank's funeral flicked through my mind. That grey sombre day, the rain, the mourners huddled together. Then Lisa's place, and her telling me about the jewellery raid. Three weeks ago. Seventy-five grand for three weeks' work. Not bad! I thought about upgrading the Beema to something even bigger, or a holiday in the Caribbean for me and Rita, and then I remembered there wasn't a Rita any more. I started thinking about her and what if anything there was to do about that.

The clock above the reception alcove said six. I wondered how much longer Stafford would be. And if he'd found any photos. With a picture of Susan's boyfriend we'd at least know who we were after. Proving it would be something else. Still, that wouldn't be my problem. Finding the drafts had been mine and I'd done that all right. I tapped my breast pocket and felt the outline of my wallet containing Saxone's receipt and allowed myself a smile of satisfaction.

I was still full of it when the front door opened and Stafford hustled in with two uniformed behind him. He stood for a moment, hands in jacket pockets, taking in the scene. I suddenly felt aroused and excited at the prospect of finding out at long last who the boyfriend was. I started to say something, he gave me a nod of recognition, then went over to the reception desk. Kamoulous stopped whistling, came to the front full of smiles and professional insincerity. Stafford shoved his warrant card under his nose.

"What's this all about, officer?" Kamoulous asked.

"Nothing to get alarmed about. I just want a word with a colleague of mine over there."

"I know. Can I be of any help? Always happy to help the cops."

Stafford came over and apologised for having taken so long. I put the fag out and asked if he'd found any photos.

"First things first, Eddie; where's the money?"

"On its way to Canary Wharf."

"Very funny! Where is it?" He led me by the elbow across the dimly lit area out of Kamoulous's and his men's hearing. "Don't piss me around, Eddie. We're talking about a lot of dough here. Where is it?"

"You're not going to like this!"

"Try me."

"Frank fenced the jewellery, not for cash but for two banker's drafts, half a mil each."

"What am I not going to like about that?"

"He hid them behind the door number plate of room twelve. They've been there for three months waiting to be found while your blokes have been in and out of that room a dozen times. As for the jewellery itself, you can whistle Dixie."

Stafford took it in. You could see it registering on his face as the lines became almost ruts at the humiliation of having been outwitted by a villain like Harvey.

"You're right, you're bloody right. I don't like it. I don't bloody like it at all. If Frank was here I'd put the little bastard in hospital." I didn't say anything. He looked at me and said, "Well, maybe not. So, where's the drafts then?"

"Allied Indemnity's bloke showed up here. So I turned them over to him. That's what I meant about being on their way to

Canary Wharf." I handed Stafford the receipt. He gave it the once-over then said,

"You'll be all right with fifteen per cent of that lot!"

"And now I've answered your questions, Chief Inspector ..."

"I know, did we get any photos?" He snapped his fingers and called one of his men to bring over the envelope he had.

"It was Terry Norton, wasn't it?" I exclaimed.

Stafford pulled the contents from the manila envelope and handed it to me. There was just one coloured print, eight by six, probably shot with something like a Canon 30D camera with a 70–200 telephoto lens. Jesus! How many times had I used one of those.

Susan was standing in a car park beside a lime-green Ford Focus. It was a bright summer day with a cloudless sky. She stood tall and slim in a cream-coloured minidress. She held a pair of sunglasses by one of its arms in her mouth while she gesticulated with her hands and looked even prettier than she had in Monica's photos. The boyfriend was there as well. A little thinner than nowadays. He wore navy trousers and a lemon half-sleeve shirt that contrasted with a deep tan. He too had sunglasses, but wore them unused on his forehead like goggles. He smiled that familiar smile of his while he held the car door open for her. I stared at the photo for a long time unable to believe what I saw and then it all sank in, and I realised what a dope I'd been. Talk about missing the bloody obvious! I turned it over but there was nothing on the back. I took another look at the image in my hand. I thought my years as a copper and then enquiry agent had hardened me against surprises and here I was, surprised. I'd been certain that if Stafford found any photos they'd be of Susan and Terry. Nothing had prepared me for this.

"Know him?" Stafford asked.

"No," I lied.

"You sure?"

"Wish I did, Chief Inspector. It would have rounded things off nicely." I wondered how I'd explain the lie tomorrow.

"Well, if it's got form, CRO'll have something." I thanked him for going to Swinburn's. "You sure you don't know him?" he asked again. "'Cause you wouldn't believe the aggro I had. They checked my warrant card about a dozen times. And still rang the nick to verify me. Rang Islington nick to send over a copper. Had me sign a statement saying it was material evidence. Then typed a receipt for the photo in which they said they were and would be responsible for absolutely nothing. It's a wonder they didn't include England being knocked out the World Cup."

I smiled blandly at his tale of tribulation while I could feel myself becoming more and more impatient, anxious to finish unfinished business.

"You should have seen …"

"Sorry to cut you short, Chief Inspector, but I've got an appointment at seven."

"Sure. I understand. I want to take a look at the door anyway."

I said I'd be in touch.

CHAPTER 36

Caxton Street was empty except for a woman walking her poodle. The early evening threatened rain. I parked the Beema outside his apartment hoping he was there, then noticed the sleek, expensive Honda Prelude. I waited until the woman had passed. A voice on my car radio interrupted some pop music to say there was a traffic hold-up on the northbound carriageway of the M4. I took my .38 from under the passanger-side carpet and checked the chambers. It felt heavier than usual, perhaps my anxiety adding to its weight. I didn't like carrying a gun, because if you do you probably end up using it. But I knew he had one, a 9 mm Smith and Wesson. He'd used it to kill Bobby and Lenny Warren and maybe others I didn't know about. I should have known it was him the moment Monica mentioned Vinnie and Don being grassed. Should have made the connection, of Don, Susan, boyfriend, insurance. It shouldn't have had to come down to seeing a photo to realise the obvious. I pressed the entryphone. That familiar voice that I hated so much asked who it was.

"British Gas. Report of a gas leak," I said in a cockney accent.

"Nothing smelling here."

"There will be in a minute if I don't check the pipe running from outside into the inside." He buzzed me in.

The entrance hall was long, had cream coloured walls, thick green carpeting and a wide sweeping staircase. There was an antique table for the post just inside the doorway, and a gilt mirror above it, stuff I'd not noticed the night we'd come back for a drink.

"Sorry to trouble you." I slipped a do-it-yourself British Gas engineer's card in the name of Kenneth Grant under his door. "I'm going to need to check your boiler. Got ID if you want. But it won't go under the door."

There was a pause. The safety chain came off. The door opened no more than a couple of inches. I kicked it so hard the force of it sent him into the hall behind him. I kicked him hard in the left shin. He bent over to tend it and as he did I kicked him in the right one, which left him doubled up.

"What the hell d'you think you're doing!" he screamed.

I closed the door and dropped the latch.

"I've come for a chat!"

He looked as dapper as ever in a light grey suit, blue shirt and navy tie, except his blond hair, always so nicely combed, was dishevelled. He could have been a doctor about to go on a house call or a stockbroker instead of a greedy little murderer. I knew now how Stafford felt when I'd told him where the drafts were, such a bloody fool.

"Jesus!" he winced, staggering and stumbling backwards along the hall.

I kicked him again. My shoe caught him square in the chest, winding him and sending him through a door into his living room and onto his backside.

"Are you fucking mad?" he yelled.

Large spots of blood appeared on his trouser legs from the kicks. He lay on the floor with a Georgian-style window for a backdrop.

"You must have had a real good laugh at my expense, Saxone! Three weeks of taking the piss and me like a dope not seeing it."

"You must be out of your mind, Sutton. I don't know what you're going on about!"

I moved across the room to a telephone sitting on a marble-topped three-legged table. I yanked the jack plug out the wall, then smashed the BT box it went into with a kick so that it couldn't be re-inserted, just in case he dived for the phone and managed 999.

He manoeuvred himself a few feet so the sofa supported his back. His face pasty white, his nice blue shirt and navy tie with a black shoe mark in the middle of it. Both trouser legs had larger stains now as more and more blood seeped into the trouser fabric. He rubbed his shins and winced.

"I'm going to kill you for this," he shrieked. He closed his eyes. He looked unable to do anything least of all kill me. "You won't get a penny from Allied, I'll see to that!"

I was sorry now I hadn't told Stafford what I knew and got assistance, because I wasn't sure where my temper might lead.

"Game's up, Saxone!"

"What game, for Chrissake!"

"I've seen the photo of you and Susan."

His face, already white with pain, drained of its remaining colour, but it was his eyes that gave him away.

"What!" But the supposed incredulity had no conviction.

"You and Susan."

"What the hell you talking about, Sutton?"

"Spare me the theatrics."

"I don't know what you're talking about."

"Course you do"

"Listen, you …"

"Cut the crap."

He tried to smile but the corner of his mouth twitched. He tried to pull himself together and get up. I kicked him again, catching him in the kneecap. He let out a scream, a real, deep-down full of pain yell, and slumped sideways. I thought he was going to pass out, but he didn't. I wondered if his neighbours might have heard him. He was the middle flat of a three-storey house, maybe, maybe not. They might not even be home. Perhaps I should have checked before ringing. What the hell! It was too late now.

"I haven't worked it all out yet. But I reckon when you heard Frank had died, you decided to have one last try at getting the jewellery, seeing how you'd invested so much time with Susan on it originally."

He said nothing. He rubbed his knee and his eyes filled with tears from the pain.

"You're going to die for this, Sutton, I swear, you're going to die for this."

"You did know Susan, didn't you?" He said nothing. Just kept rubbing his knee. "Course you did. You made a mistake not telling me you'd met Don Taylor through the Barlow House investigation. That's how you first came to meet her, isn't it, investigating Don and the robbery?"

"Why won't you believe me; I don't know what you're on about!"

" Don told her her about the proposed raid and the double cross. He'd have had to. If he was going to rehearse her for what to say if the police came calling.Especially if he was going to trust her for an alibi. And you and she saw your chance.So much for trust!"I remembered my drink with Stafford in the pub. He was right. It was about a triple cross. "Then you joined forces with Bobby, or maybe you and he were already mates. Then for some reason you decided to kill him. Why? Scared he'd spill everything to me when we met at Poland Street?"

"And how was I supposed to know the two of you were meeting, eh?"

"You tapped his phone."

He shook his head.

"Rubbish!"

"You tapped mine. You've probably hacked my mobile as well, because I removed the bug from my phone after I realised you'd been in my office."

He sat there listening, taking it all in that he'd been rumbled.

"Of course! You've hacked my mobile; that's how you knew to be at the Parkland that day Lisa and I searched it. That's why you were there this afternoon. Because you heard me call her, and Tom

Stafford. That must have put you in quite a dilemma. Either get to Swinburn's before Stafford and get the photo if they'd let you have it, that's assuming there was one. Or intercept me in case I decided not to cough up the drafts."

There's a point in a criminal interview sometimes when your position supported by the facts becomes so overwhelmingly obvious and logical it crumbles the interviewee's resistance and resolve for further lies. We must have reached that point, or maybe he just couldn't handle a further beating, because he suddenly nodded.

"You did kill Bobby, didn't you?"

"Necessity, laddie. I let slip when I interviewed him after Frank's funeral that Susan planned to run off with someone to Spain the weekend of the raid." I didn't see the connection until he said, "It's only something Susan's boyfriend could have known. He started digging around. He got hold of a snap of me and her and planned to get one from Warren. He said unless I shared the money with him he'd grass me to you and Allied. Well, I wasn't going to share, and I wasn't going to be blackmailed ..." The sentence trailed off.

"You killed Lenny too, didn't you?"

He nodded, and nodded, and nodded, and just kept nodding, like all resistance was spent.

"I hacked a phone call from Warren to Bobby, who told him he'd followed Susan, not Lisa and that he might have a photo of the two of us. I went to see Warren; I asked for the photo. He said he didn't have it, then he started attacking me."

I didn't believe a word of it because Lenny had stopped one right between the eyes sitting in one of his PVC chairs.

The room felt oppressively hot. I could have opened a window, but I might have been tempted to throw him out of it.

"Where are the drafts?" I asked.

He wiped his mouth with the back of his hand and left a smear of blood on his cheek and across his nose.

"In the office safe."

"Liar! You wouldn't have had time to get from Finsbury Park to the City to here. Besides, you're not going to surrender them to Allied. You were somehow going to get the receipt back from me, weren't you? How? Kill me too? Then sell the drafts on, to someone who can do something with them. Someone who'd know how to use them given they're made out to Frank and Don, and not you. Four hundred thousand, maybe half a mil? It's better than nothing!"

"I'll do a deal with you, Sutton."

I grabbed hold of him by his hair and dragged him across the floor towards the door.

"You just don't get it, do you? It's over. I want the drafts and then I'm out of here." I went through his jacket pockets, keys, mobile, wallet; I threw the lot across the room. "I'm not leaving without them even if I have to put you in a coma." I wondered where he'd have them. I pulled him to his feet and pushed him down the hall. He limped, half-stumbled. "Where's your coat?" I pulled open a hall cupboard. There was a hanging rail. But nothing hanging from it. There was a shelf above with some towels and a polythene bag underneath. I pulled the lot down. The bag hit the carpet and Saxone's electrical voltage toy and some handcuffs spilled out of it.

He suddenly rammed me into the cupboard, then nutted me. I lashed out but he smashed the cupboard door into my face. My nose started bleeding. My head felt leaden. I shook it trying to clear the pain. There was a flash of white and I realised too late the door had been swung again, this time right into me. He tried to reach for the bag but I pushed him off, then kicked him hard in one of his already wounded shins. His howl reverberated throughout the entire flat. Then I kicked him in the bollocks, and that was that. He lay there still. I wasn't sure if he was conscious or not. I waited a few moments and he started groaning. I dragged him by his collar to a central heating radiator and handcuffed him to the pipes. Then I slumped on the floor propped against the wall, absolutely drained. The blood felt salty in my mouth. There were gobs of it on my shirt and my arm ached like hell from taking the force of the cupboard door. Saxone lay hunched, his face turned to the opposite wall, breathing heavily, but otherwise motionless.

I found the bathroom. I rinsed my mouth and splashed my face, then went back to him and plugged in his electrical box of tricks. He didn't move or speak, but I knew he knew what was coming.

"I don't have time to waste. So I'm going to start with the dial at ten." That nasty, menacing, vicious hum filled the air. Saxone tried to wrench the pipe he was secured around, but nothing gave. "I don't need to tell you how we play this game, do I?" He tried the pipe again. "Worst way if you won't talk, I'll sellotape the fucking wires to you then tear the place apart."

"The drafts are in my bedroom," he gasped. "The drafts are in my bedroom! In my coat, on the bed!"

His bedroom was next to the bathroom. It was large. In the centre of it was a king-size bed mounted on a black carpeted plinth, with black satin sheets and mirrored ceiling tiles. His coat, a long camel-coloured cashmere job, lay on the bed. The drafts were in the inside pocket, in a white envelope. I came back to him, pulled the plug out of the wall, dropped the handcuff keys just out of his reach, then closed the front door behind me.

CHAPTER 37

I sat in my car, pulled a hip flask of brandy from the glove compartment and took a long belt. It washed the remains of the salt taste out of my mouth and the ache out of my arm. I checked the safety was on the .38, pleased I hadn't had to use it, and stuck it back under the carpet. It was dark now, the sodium street lights cast irregular shadows over the pavement. Images jumped in my mind — me kicking Saxone, him nutting me and slamming the cupboard door on me, and the little coward shit-scared of his own torture toy being used on him. I'd phone Stafford to give him the SP on Saxone. I owed him for his help. But tomorrow or the next day, because there were things to do and he might prevent me from doing them.

I took another nip when my mobile rang. It was Lisa in tears.

"What's wrong?" I asked.

"George and Terry's just been here," she sniffed.

"And?"

"They was looking for you." There was a long pause. She blew her nose. "They went back to the B&B for another search. Kamoulous told them we'd been there and Saxone, and the police, and he thought you'd found something. They went to your place, couldn't find you and turned up here."

"What d'you tell them?" She hesitated and began sobbing again. "Lisa?"

"I tried not to say anything, honest! But Terry hit me. Then George ripped my shirt open. Eddie, he said he was going to put me across my dining room table and teach me a lesson I'd never forget. I had to tell them. That you'd found the drafts and handed them over to the insurance agent."

"What did they say?"

"That they're going to blow your legs off!"

"You okay now?"

She sniffed again, and sighed.

"Sort of. I'm going to spend the night at a girlfriend's."

"Good."

"What you gonna do, Eddie?"

"I'm not sure."

"They're a pair of nutters. Especially George. He went mental when I told him."

"How long ago was this?"

"They've just left."

"Did they say where they were going?"

"No. But my guess is back to you. Where are you?"

"West London."

"What you gonna do?"

"Have a drink!"

And that's exactly what I did, taking another belt from the hip flask. It had all seemed so easy to start with. Get the drafts. Hand them over to the insurance company and split the reward. And now things were out of hand. Bobby was dead. Lenny too. I'd been at a murder scene and might be identified as a suspect. The drafts had blood on them. The insurance investigator was guilty of conspiracy to rob, to pervert the course of justice, to defraud, oh, and did I mention murder? And as soon as Allied found out, it was as certain they'd distance themselves from Saxone and completely blank Lisa and me as far as a reward was concerned. So all my efforts would have been for nothing. And on top of all that, George Norton wanted to kill me!

I lit a ciggie, and blew smoke at the night. I toyed with the alternatives, but nothing seemed satisfactory. The obvious was to take George's hundred grand, or Terry's one two five and call it a day. But, realistically, neither of their offers was an option. It left me vulnerable to blackmail and once the drafts were in their hands, I'd have no more control over matters, and if they should get done for receiving and dealing in stolen goods, so would I. I closed my eyes and lay back in the seat and tried again, and then I had a brainwave and dialled Steve.

"It's Eddie."

"How you doing?"

"Got a bit of bother. I want to borrow your back room." I checked my watch; it was nearly 8 p.m. "About 10 p.m. this evening."

"What for?"

"A meet."

"No problem."

"I'll need you with me."

"For how long? I've got an empire to run."

"Twenty minutes, max."

"See you when I see you."

I hung up and rang Lisa who said she was just on her way to her friend. Her voice was still shaky. But she sounded as though the tears had passed. I asked if George or Terry would know where her friend lived; she said no. I told her to stay with the friend for a couple of nights.

"What's going on?" she asked.

"Just a bit of aggro to sort. If you think you're being followed by them this evening, go to Steve's Snooker Hall, 1798 Kilburn High Road. If not, go to your friend and stay there until I ring you." She asked again what was going on. "If I don't see you by ten, I'll assume you're at your friend's."

"Why d'you want to get rid of me?"

"I don't want the Nortons kidnapping you."

"Shit! You serious?"

"Very. Speak to you in a couple of days."

I pulled out the slip of paper Terry had given me and dialled. George answered.

"It's Eddie Sutton."

"You got some fucking front ringing me." I could hear Terry in the background asking who it was. George told him. "I'm gonna blow your legs off, Sutton."

"No, you won't."

"Wanna bet! I hear you did a deal with the insurance people."

"Is that right? So what am I holding in my hand? It's not my dick."

"I want those fucking drafts! Where are you?"

"Not so fast." I threw the cigarette out of the window and slid my seat back. "Situation's changed, George."

"Is that right?"

"Turns out the drafts aren't going to be much use to either of us. Well, not at the moment."

"How d'you make that out?"

"They're made out to Frank and Don. Make a mistake in who you sell them on to, now that Bobby and Lenny Warren are dead, it'll all come back on you like pissing in a wind tunnel."

"So what you gonna do? Frame them and hang them in your lav?"

"No. I've got a better idea."

"And what's that, Einstein?" I could hear him moving his phone around and I guessed it was so that Terry could hear the conversation.

"Going to get you some dough. Me some dough, and me off the hook with you."

"How?"

"Meet me at 10 p.m. tonight at Steve's snooker hall."

George started laughing, which ended in a deep, rasping smoker's cough.

"What's so funny?"

"You're taking the piss, right?"

172

"Meaning?"

"Me and Terry turn up at this club, get croaked and you have it off with them drafts."

"Don't flatter yourself. You're not worth doing twenty-five years for, believe me. Stafford knows I had the drafts, he knows you're after them. When he checks my phone records and sees that I spoke to you less than two hours before you supposedly got done, you don't need to be Sherlock Holmes to know who'd be the prime suspect, do you?" There was silence for a few moments while he mulled over what I hoped made common sense.

"Where's this snooker hall then?" he asked.

"Terry'll tell you, won't you, Terry, 'cause you've been there recently, haven't you!"

I put the mobile away. The lights were still on in Saxone's flat. Maybe he'd go into hiding, or skip the country. Arrogant little bastard like him might even stay put and front the whole thing out. It didn't matter. One call to Stafford tomorrow or the next day once my interests had been satisfied and Saxone would be exit stage right permanently.

CHAPTER 38

I went home, showered, changed clothes and got to Steve's at about 9.30 p.m. Most of the tables were occupied. There were the usual sounds, laughter, coughing, swearing, the TV in the background and the occasional clanking of coins as a fruit machine paid out.The room was at the back of the hall. It had a desk, several visitors' chairs and a brown-patterned sofa along one wall where paint flaked from the damp. There was a lime-green Venetian blind over the window. It was a bland anonymous room, probably a stockroom turned into an office. Steve had put a bottle of Scotch and a few glasses on a coffee table near the chairs.

"I thought you might want a drink while you were doing business," he said.

"It's not that sort of meeting. The Nortons are coming round."

"Because of those draft things? What happened by the way?" I told him. He shook his head in disbelief. "You said you needed help."

I gave him my .38.

"I want you to sit in on the meeting. Don't do or say anything. Nothing. Just sit there, but if I scratch my nose like this," and I ran my thumb and finger down it, "pull the gun and point it at George and give him a serious eyeballing."

"And that's it?"

"That's it!"

"What if he's carrying?"

"You look mean enough; he'll think twice about pulling it."

Steve checked the safety was on, then slipped it under his shirt and into his trouser waistband.

"I'll be behind the bar. I'll bring them over when they turn up."

It was 10 p.m. Punters drifted in and out. But no sign of the Nortons. By 10.15 p.m. I was thinking they wouldn't show, when the black guy that had beaten me up in my flat that night with George walked in. He looked this way and that, then behind him at the door he'd just come through. He was bigger than I remembered. He wore jeans and trainers, a blue check shirt and a body warmer. I eyed him carefully, but it didn't look as though he was carrying. He exchanged a few words with Steve who pointed towards me, and then he made his way over. He looked around as he walked. He brushed past me into the office without speaking, looked around it then pulled a mobile.

"It's me, it's cool!" and clicked off. "You can't take chances these days," he said to me sitting astride a chair, "there's just so many villains around." Another time I'd have smiled.

Five minutes later, George, in black trousers and long, black leather coat, came in with Terry wearing those granny sunglasses which made me think it was a wonder he could see where he was walking. Steve recognised Terry, made the connection. He said something to little Harry, his help, then beckoned the Nortons to follow. Neither said hello. They pulled the chairs over towards the door. Steve closed it and both he and I sat on the sofa. I asked if they wanted a drink. All three refused.

"Who's this?" George asked nodding towards Steve.

"A friend. He stays."

"So?" George said. I looked at the black guy, then at George. "Darren's okay."

"It's like I said on the phone. I've got the drafts. But there's a problem."

"We had a deal, Sutton!"

"You had a deal! The first problem is that the drafts aren't in either of our names."

"That's no snag. I know people."

175

"The second is. They could become evidence in a murder enquiry."

"Still no snag. 'Cause it's not my problem."

"Mine either. Because I've thought of an answer to both."

"Well, that's the foreplay, now get to the fucking!"

"What would you get if you traded them? Forty pence in the pound?"

"Fifty."

"That's half a mil. Suppose I can get you eight hundred thousand?"

"Bloody brilliant!" Terry exclaimed.

George shot him a look and he blanched at his own indiscretion.

"I'm listening," George said.

"The drafts came from a Belgium diamond company that worked a stroke making the jewellery disappear and funding Frank's pay-off. That incidentally was why he got paid in drafts as opposed to cash. Because they made the whole thing look legal."

"So?"

"We get them to exchange the drafts for cash."

"Really! And what do we do when they tell us to piss off? Sue them?"

"No. We tell them we've got nothing to lose. We'll grass them and Ralph to the authorities. Customs and Excise can trace those drafts back to source. Which would open a can of worms that would finish them. They'd have to agree to cover themselves and protect future deals." I waited for George to say something. But he didn't. "Besides," I added, "they've nothing to lose. It's a million for a million."

He sat there turning it over in his mind. He crossed his legs, stroked his chin, helped himself to some Scotch. And at last said,

"What about the other problem? Them being evidence and all that?"

"I've got a receipt for the drafts from the insurance agent. As far as I'm concerned I handed them over to him, he's still got them, anybody wants them, talk to him." And given, I was going to add but didn't, that by the time any of this came to light he'd be on trial for murder, who's going to believe anything he says anyway.

You could tell the taste for eight hundred grand was going around and around in his head, because he only just succeeded in suppressing a smile.

"How d'you manage to get the drafts and the receipt? Or is that asking!"

"Like you once said to me, I can be very persuasive when I try."

"And how d'you make it eight hundred? A mil less a oner is nine hundred grand."

"That was on yesterday's market. I'd say I was worth more than a hundred grand. Wouldn't you agree, Terry?" But Terry didn't reply. "They give us two suitcases. One with eight hundred grand in. That's yours. Another, with two hundred in. That's mine. And that's it! I'm off the hook with you. Goodbye, good luck, it's been lovely knowing you, end of story!"

He finished his drink and put the glass on the carpet beside the chair.

"Of course, there is another way round all this," he said. "I come over to your place later, break your legs or worse, and take the drafts."

I wondered if he thought he'd frighten me. He hadn't, because it wasn't anything less than I'd been expecting.

"If I don't ring a friend of mine tomorrow morning to say I'm okay, he rings Stafford with your names and all the details. Then Steve here and a couple of my mates'll be waiting for you one evening outside your yard. You and Terry'll be dead before you can lock the gates." I scratched my nose. Steve pulled the gun and pointed it at George. He held him eyeball to eyeball with the meanest look I'd ever seen until George backed down first and looked away. "Right between the eyes. Either Steve here, or another pal, before you've even locked the gates." Even if he had a gun, I don't think he'd have pulled it.

"I can certainly see the strength of your argument," he said sarcastically.

"So, we're agreed? Let me put it this way." I pulled the drafts out of my pocket and held them above a Zippo lighter. "Say yes. You get eight hundred grand. Say no. I burn the fucking things now. Because you're not worth doing a stretch for!"

He had to say yes. What else could he say! And he did. I put the drafts away. Steve rested the gun in his lap with his finger around the trigger, but continued to give George the stare. He hadn't blinked once since pulling the shooter. Darren suddenly stood up. Steve turned the gun on him.

"I'm just getting myself some Scotch. Be cool! We're all friends now, remember." He lifted the bottle. "Terry?" Terry tried to say yes but the word stuck in his throat and he just nodded.

"So you and me, George. We go to Leyton's tomorrow 9.30 a.m. and tell him to arrange things for the following night. Right?"

"Right!" he replied. He jerked his head at the other two. "We're out of here," he said, and they were.

I watched them go, then poured us doubles. Steve handed me back my gun and let out a long low whistle.

"You got some balls, Eddie boy." He stretched back on the sofa and drank some of his Scotch. "You're lucky a lunatic like that didn't tell you to burn the drafts and go fuck yourself." He finished his drink was at the door when he said, "Just out of curiosity. Would you have burnt them?"

"These? Oh yes, they're only photocopies!"

178

CHAPTER 39

George burst into Leyton's shop, got hold of him by his shirt and rammed him up against a wall. It happened so quickly neither Leyton nor I took it in for the moment. He then swung Leyton round and shoved him up against an opposite wall so hard that the jewellery in a showcase beside him jumped, and if George hadn't held him in his fist I think he'd have slumped to the floor.

"Get out. I'll call the police!" Leyton yelled. "Police, police, someone help!"

Norton called for me to close the door and put the 'Closed' sign on. He dragged Leyton down the shop and dumped him in a chair behind a partition that screened him from the street.

"Sit down, shut up, and speak when you're spoken to," he said.

I wondered what all the violence was about because the blackmail was going to do the trick. Maybe it was violence he'd like to have meted out to me. Leyton winced as he rubbed his arm, then his body.

"I got no money. Only the float." He looked at me and it registered who we were and that this wasn't petty villainy.

George bent over him so they were inches apart. I'd never realised before just how intimidating he was, even weaponless, when right in your face.

"We want you to phone your mates in Belgium 'cause we got a message for them."

"Belgium?"

"Don't piss me around. We've got Frank Harvey's drafts. We're gonna do a swap. A million worth of drafts for a million worth of readies."

"Impossible."

179

George looked around and found a phone and dropped it in Leyton's lap. Ralph pulled his top pocket handkerchief out and mopped his forehead.

"Get dialling, old man!"

"You, you don't understand!"

"Do it!" Norton yelled.

Leyton shook his head.

"I have to ring Hatton Garden. Nobody in Belgium will speak to me."

"Who in Hatton Garden?" I asked.

"My contact."

"What's his name?" George wouldn't even stand for a couple of seconds' hesitation. "Name!" he yelled, so ferociously even I was taken aback.

"Stanton, Ben Stanton."

Ralph pulled a little pocketbook from the inside of his jacket, turned a few pages and croaked out the number. I wrote it down, George dialled, then gave him the receiver.

"Ben, it's Ralph. There's trouble."

I took the receiver from him and said,

"Lots of trouble actually." Stanton asked who I was. He had a very deep, self-assured voice. I guessed he was middling fifties. "I'm part of the firm on the Kensington business." George shot me a look, then went back to watching Leyton. "We've got the drafts you used to pay Frank with. We don't want them. We want the dough instead."

"Meaning?"

"A swap. Drafts for money."

"Go fuck yourself!"

"Or else."

"Or else what?"

"We spill the lot to the cops."

"You can still go fuck yourself! You've got nothing except the drafts."

"What we've got is a company in Belgium that buys bent gear with banker's drafts, gets moody invoices from a company in Liechtenstein that probably doesn't exist for a quarter of the stock. Re-cuts twenty-five per cent of the stuff and puts it into inventory supported by the invoice, then it sells the balance under the counter. What we've got is drafts drawn on Banque Nationale de Belgique made out to two known villains, one shot dead by police at the site of a jewellery raid in Kensington, the other was on remand for said raid, with a serial number in the top left-hand corner that the DTI, Customs and Excise, The Serious Crime Squad and my fucking granny could trace. What we've got is your name and number and a sixty-year-old known fence who'll give you up before doing ten. And if we don't have an exchange at 7 p.m. tomorrow night, it's what Tom Stafford, a DCI at Kensington nick, will have."

There was silence for a long time. I thought he'd hung up when he said,

"I'll have to make some phone calls." This time his voice didn't sound so self-assured. "We'll need more than thirty-four hours."

"You got thirty-four hours. Actually, thirty-three hours and forty-eight minutes. We want eight hundred grand in one suitcase. And two hundred in a different coloured one. I'll contact Leyton tomorrow morning with the swap arrangements." I looked over at Ralph, who sat with his head in his hands. "You taking this in, Stanton?" I asked.

"Yes. Eight in one. Two in another."

"Good. Because if your people don't perform, you'd best take a permanent holiday."

"I want to speak to Ralph." I put him back on.

"Yes, yes," Ralph said. "They pushed me around, but I'm okay." He looked up at me and George and said, "Yes. Very serious." He said goodbye and replaced the receiver.

I asked him for his number. His face was red, strands of grey hair hung in his eyes. He rubbed his arm again, then sat back hugging himself as he rocked back and forth on the chair.

CHAPTER 40

George leaned against his Merc and lit a cigar. He'd parked up on the kerb and the fact that it restricted the view of pedestrians crossing the road or the view of drivers coming out of a side turning didn't seem to bother him. I thought he'd offer me one. I should have known better.

"Getting a bit previous in there, weren't you?" he said, "giving Stanton all that verbal and making arrangements off your own back."

"He told me to go fuck myself. So I gave him something to think about."

He drew on his cigar and the flame on the lighter flared.

"You know they're going to try and do us in, don't you?" he said, puffing a plume of smoke.

"Maybe. Maybe they'll settle for the easy way out. We're holding all the cards."

"Trust me! They're probably on the phone now plotting something. Won't do them no good though. Ever done a trade-off before?"

"Once. To recover a stolen painting. You?"

"A few. You just have to look hard and keep your nerve."

"What kind of circumstances?"

"You don't wanna know." Which I guess meant drug deals or a kidnapping. "So. To business. There's a piece of waste ground just off Marsh Lane in Catford. One way in, same way out. Not much built-up ground, so nowhere for snipers to hide. We go tooled up, mob-handed. Me, Terry, Darren. You, that geezer with the shooter last night, and AN Other."

"Not so fast, George." He yanked the cigar out of his mouth in a fit of pique. The lips pulled back in a snarl. Even the hint of a challenge to his authority was enough to test his patience. "I'll take a look and let you know."

He pulled a deliberate false smile.

"Assuming it meets with your agreement," he said sarcastically. "We line our motors up side by side ten, fifteen feet apart. Me and Terry in front of mine what's-his-name?"

"Steve."

"Steve, you and one other in front of yours. Shooters ready."

"What about Darren?"

"He's on the floor in the back of my car in case anyone gets ideas. Then you and Terry, and their two, meet halfway between the two sets of motors. When we've done the swap we get in our cars and we're out of it like lightning. Piece of piss really, unless someone gets trigger-happy."

"It won't be me."

"Good. Let's hope it's not them either. Because if anyone so much as farts I'll start blasting. You got my word on it!"

"This your vehicle, sir?" We turned around to find a traffic warden, minicomputer in hand.

"No. It's David Cameron's. He's just gone across the road to McDonald's for a piss. He asked me to keep an eye out for him for any evil fucking traffic wardens."

"D'you mind moving it, please."

"Certainly. Would you like another couple of seconds to look at it 'cause that's nearest you'll ever get to owning one!" He got in and started up. He lowered the window and said to me, "Don't get any ideas about tomorrow night, Sutton. Pull something that's not in the script, I'll blow you away." He pulled out into the traffic and took off.

CHAPTER 41

I didn't even go to Marsh Lane, because it was George's suggestion. I phoned him and said we'd be using a place at the end of Rawlins Street behind Hackney Downs station in North East London. He didn't like it. I didn't think he would. Then I phoned Leyton and told him we'd be there at 7 p.m.

The spot was a vacant piece of waste ground on the other side of the railway line accessed from a single through road. It was separated from the tracks by high, grey concrete slab partitioning, topped with barbed wire. It was land due for redevelopment according to a large yellow and black estate agent's hoarding. '3 impressive s/c light industrial units of approx. 2000 sq ft each due Spring 2015.' But at the moment all there was to be seen were two small two-storey derelict flat-roofed sheds. All the windows smashed, their frames rotting, the brickwork crumbling, and all about them rusting water tanks and abandoned piping. There were tyre tracks in the road and oil rainbows in the puddles. It was still light, just, at least for a while — long enough!

I turned off the ignition, took a sip of Scotch, then handed the flask to Steve, who took a belt, then passed it back to Ritchie Newton, a friend of ours. Ritchie had been a useful middleweight until one night someone more useful had given him a detached retina and ended his career. Nowadays he fought in unlicensed bouts and debt collected for a loan shark. He was still slim, with cauliflower ears, stumpy nose and an ever-present sour expression, just right to make up the numbers.Ritchie had hardly put the flask to his lips when George's Merc glided its way through the puddles, U-turned and pulled up about fifteen feet away. All five of us got out of our cars.

"You all right, Darren?" George asked, without turning around.

"Shooter in one hand, can of lager in the other. Why wouldn't I be?" came the reply from the floor of the car.

George looked Ritchie up and down and gave him the slightest of nods as a hello. Then looked around at the starkness of the place.

"Marsh Lane would have been better," he said to no one in particular. He didn't look at all nervous. "Check the sheds and the hoarding, Terry." Terry pulled a shotgun off the front seat and walked off. "Seven right?" George said. "What time you got?"

"Five to."

He walked over to my car, looked through the open window, tried the boot, then looked underneath it.

Terry ambled back and nodded at George. They both got back in the Merc. Me, Steve and Ritchie got in the Beema.

"Reckon George'll try something?" Steve asked.

"Don't know. Best be ready though." He leaned over and took a pump-action shotgun from the back seat and laid it beside him.

I breathed on the windscreen and wrote '200K' in the condensation, then wiped it away. There'd be plenty of time later to think about the money. A train up the line whistled and minutes later rattled past us. The road fell silent again. George got out of his car and leaned against the door. Terry absent-mindedly rubbed his chin up and down the barrel of his shotgun. He smiled, perhaps at something Darren said in the darkness behind him. I wondered how many of them there would be and if six of us would be enough.

It was two minutes past seven when they swung onto the plot and pulled up thirty-odd feet from us. They were in a green Cherokee Jeep, headlights unnecessarily on, the light reflecting on the shiny bull bars. We got out of our cars and spread ourselves across the front of the motors, everyone except George holding a shooter. The jeep rolled another few feet forward and stopped. The headlights were killed and ordinary, early evening light resumed. Norton

186

ambled towards them slowly, very slowly, his black stubbled face expressionless, his hands at his sides I guessed to show he wasn't carrying, although it was as sure as hell he had a piece tucked away. He and the driver exchanged words.

Their doors opened and six of them with shotguns got out. The wheelman, who was about seven foot, blond and wore jeans and a zip-up, jerked his head and his mates spread themselves. Another walked around the back of the vehicle and reappeared with two suitcases. My heart started pounding and great gobs of sweat began rolling from my armpits. I took another nip of Scotch to lubricate my mouth, then dropped the flask through the open window of my car. George walked backwards towards us.

"You and Terry walk slowly to the mid-spot. Two of them'll bring up the cases. You two," he said to Steve and Ritchie, but to Darren as well, "they start anything funny shoot first, think about it later." He stood there like a little South London Napoleon in a black leather coat organising things. The trouble was he was right, and now there was no going back.

The Scotch began to kick in. I put my gun in the car beside my hip flask and took the drafts from my pocket. Terry handed his shotgun to George and we started walking towards them. I took some deep breaths. My senses were alive but less jangled by the adrenalin than they had been thanks to the alcohol. The light breeze ruffled my hair and dried the sweat on my forehead. The opposition were splayed right out. Five of them, looking almost embossed on a background of shitty wasteland in the last light of day. The blond guy was back in the jeep, drumming all eight fingers on the steering wheel in time to the throb of the engine.

"Don't worry, Sutton," Terry whispered from the corner of his mouth, "I got enough guns in my waistband to have fought El Alamein on my own."

Their two were as tall as the driver, but much beefier. One had black crew cut-cropped hair, the other was shaven headed, his scalp covered with a bluey-grey hue where the hair had been. They looked like wrestlers, or bouncers. They each carried a case, both black, but one with a whitewashed 'X' on the lid. I shot a quick look over my shoulder as I reached the midway point. George, Steve and Ritchie stood across the width of the cars ready for business. I kept looking, alert for trouble that could come from anywhere. Trying to see it, hear it, feel it before it happened. The dark cropped-haired one took the case from his mate and put them both on the ground. He flipped the locks, and I flinched at the sound of them opening.

The case with the whitewashed lid had sixteen piles of fifty-pound notes. I picked up several at random and fanned through them, I guessed there was about a thousand in a pile. I checked as far as possible, albeit in a limited way, that the notes had different serial numbers and when I rubbed them no ink came off on my fingers. So they didn't appear to be forgeries. The two of them exchanged quick glances as I grabbed a bundle from right at the bottom to see that the money wasn't bulked out with newspaper or telephone directories. I pulled the other case over. There was also sixteen piles of fifties. But about half the thickness of the bundles in the first case. I examined those as well. They seemed okay. I nodded at Terry and asked him if he wanted to take a look. He said yes. And squatted down and went through the same procedure. Their two exchanged glances again.

"Looks okay to me!" Terry said.

The shaven-headed one moved closer.

"Drafts!" he said in a continental accent. I handed them over. "I'm going to put hand in jacket, bring out envelope. Okay?"

"So long as that's all you bring out," Terry replied.

He pulled out the envelope and took a piece of paper from it and compared it with the drafts. Then he slowly pulled a small magnifying glass out. I couldn't understand why my breathing had become so difficult. Until I realised I wasn't breathing, I'd been holding my breath. I took in a couple of deep lungfuls of air and tried to relax a little. Maybe they didn't want any trouble after all, I told myself, and then I remembered what George had said, 'You know they're gonna try and do us in, don't you?' and a surge of adrenalin spurted through my brain, making the deep breathing a waste of time. Their man ran his glass slowly over one of the drafts, held it up to the fading light, then rubbed his finger over it. He licked the corner of it and rubbed it again. Then he did exactly the same with the other draft.

"All's okay," he said.

I bent down slowly, my eyes on him, felt for the case lids and closed them. I handed the one with the 'X' to Terry. The continental guy put the drafts in the envelope with the other stuff and stuck it in his pocket. Then he and his mate started walking backwards towards their motor. As we did to ours. I held the case one-handed in front of me so it could be raised as a shield if firing started. A two-hundred-grand shield! I wondered if a bullet could penetrate all those banknotes. It seemed too easy. I shook the thought from my head, not wanting paranoia and adrenalin to get the better of me.

"It's been a piece of piss," Terry whispered.

"You're not home yet!"

The bald guy and his mate were at the jeep. He opened the door at the back and the pair got in. A side window opened and they poked shotguns out giving cover to the rest of their crew as they got in. The motor rolled towards us a few yards then U-turned away. You could just see the tail lights and hear the sound of their engine as I got back to my car. Ritchie and Steve stood by, guns ready in anticipation of aggro from the Nortons. I wondered how long we'd been at it. I guessed the better part of an hour. I looked at my watch, seven and a half minutes! I retrieved my hip flask and took a belt. George took the case from Terry, put it on the roof of the Merc and opened it.

"Eight hundred grand. Nice one! I must be getting old."

"Why's that?" I asked.

"I was expecting trouble, big time."

"So was Sutton," Terry said, "that's why he nearly shit himself over there!"

"You know, we really must have a proper chat, you and me, some time, Terry," I replied.

CHAPTER 42

It sounded like a firecracker. I didn't have time to truly see where the sound had come from before Ritchie was slammed by the force of the bullet against the Merc. He lay on the ground, propped against the car. He held his chest, then looked at his hands, red from his own blood as were his shirt and trousers. He closed his eyes like he just was taking a nap gently, quietly, and he was dead. Terry turned towards the sound. There was a quizzical look on his face. It took him a second or two to realise the situation. He raised his shotgun, but two seconds was too long. A bullet hit him on the bridge of the nose. Bone, blood and mucous splattered different ways making his face look like the inside of a pomegranate. He let out a wailing yell that reverberated over the waste ground, got off a round and dropped dead too.

Steve was already diving for cover when the ricochet caught him on the side of the head and spun him round. He went over awkwardly, cracking his temple. I felt my stomach drop away at the sight of him lying there. I wanted to help him. But George grabbed my arm.

"What the fuck's going on?" he yelled, his face pasty white even behind stubble.

"Me," someone shouted, "that's what!"

I knew the voice. But couldn't believe what I heard. He came limping out of the shadows of the gathering dusk, holding what looked like an automatic rifle. He'd fired three rounds so there were plenty more and even if it was only semi-automatic, at twenty-odd feet he'd have enough time not to miss.

"Hands in the air where I can see them."

I raised mine slowly. I kept looking over at Steve, trying to see movement, but there was none. George raised his hands and said,

"Who the fuck are you?"

"His name's Brian Saxone, and he's going to kill us."

"He's right on both points," Saxone replied with a smile.

"Why?"

"Because the bastard's got a taste for it. Look around." The lights suddenly came on over the railway tracks, bathing everything in an orange glow. "He was Susan's boyfriend, the reason Frank hid the drafts, Bobby's killer and now he's killed my best friend." I wanted to add, sorry I hadn't wasted him the other evening in his flat.

George shook his head in disbelief then caught sight of his brother's faceless body splayed in the mud. He closed his eyes and you could see a lump come up in his throat and I knew exactly how he felt.

Saxone circled us awkwardly, holding the rifle at shoulder level.

"Over there by the wall."

We moved to the grey concrete partitioning.

"How d'you know to be here?" I asked. "I pulled the bug out of my phone days ago."

He smiled that evil little smile of his, then vanity got the better of him.

"I bugged an extension in another room of Leyton's flat just before you got there that night while I had him strapped. It's not been touched. I heard everything yesterday when you rang to make the swap arrangements. I've been waiting on the roof of one of those sheds." He paused as though waiting for us to congratulate him on his prowess. "All that remains," he continued, "is for me to get rid of you two and voilà! I go back to work on Monday like nothing's happened, but a million pounds richer."

"I suppose there's no point in telling you you're insane?"

"Norton, yours will be quick. But I got plans for Sutton." He opened his body warmer so I could see the butt of the Smith and Wesson in his trouser waistband. "One in each kneecap. Then a kicking, I mean a really good kicking. Then one in the bollocks, then when I think you've had enough pain, one between the eyes."

"No, I thought not!"

"That's right, Sutton!" George said. "He's gonna kill us and you're making jokes. And you say he's nuts! Oi, Saxone, or whatever your name is. Do Sutton if you want, who cares! But we can work something out. There's a million quid over there and I've got nearly a quarter of a mil in unmarked readies in my safe at the yard, that's a million and a quarter. Just like that! We just open the safe and it's yours, Bob's your uncle!"

"I don't do partnerships, laddie. I'm a sole trader."

"I'm serious. Quarter of a mil in cash. It's yours, I promise you, it's yours, it's yours! Don't do this!"

It was the first time I'd ever seen George really frightened.

Saxone circled us keeping the rifle trained. But he began moving in a line towards the Merc. From the corner of my eye, I mean right from the furthest field of vision, I could just make out the tip of the barrel of Darren's shotgun poking out the window. It was such a temptation to turn, I had to dig my fingernails into my palms to remain focused on Saxone. The barrel moved a bit. Saxone ordered us further back, I supposed so that it might take longer for our bodies to be discovered rather than left in the middle of the plot. The barrel followed him. I hoped Darren wasn't drunk from all the lager he'd been swilling. I needn't have worried. He fired so many times he emptied the shotgun, boom after boom after boom. Two rounds hit Saxone in the back throwing him forward making him lurch, then stumble like a puppet being yanked by a rope. Another hit him in the head, blood and fluid spat out as half his scalp flew off and down he went.

George and I dived away from the line of fire. He to the left, me to the right. I huddled against the stone parapet, my hands over my head concerned for ricochets. I waited for half a minute or so in case Darren was up for an encore. There was no question he'd killed Saxone. I just hoped it had been incredibly painful.

"Nice one, Darren!" George yelled, his voice carrying on the echo of the gunfire.

I sat up against the slabbing to find him and Darren holding guns on me. I held out my hand expecting to be pulled up. They both stepped backwards. Darren fixed another magazine in his shotgun. George had picked up the one belonging to Saxone, who lay face down, with blood, looking like chocolate sauce under the orange lighting, oozing from a large head wound and soaking into the ground.

"Change of plan," George said to me.

"Oh?"

"'Fraid so."

"We had a deal."

"You had a deal. I've decided to liquidate the partnership, and one of the partners, as it 'appens."

A little way over to my left I suddenly noticed Steve moving. He shook his head, then tried to move, said,

"Fuck it" and struggled to sit up.

Even with George holding a gun on me, I couldn't contain my smile. His face and shirt were covered with blood from a wound at the side of his head. It still bled and what wasn't soaking into his hair dripped everywhere, but it didn't matter because he was alive.

"What happened?" he asked. He tried to straighten himself and fell backwards. He closed his eyes, I thought he'd gone. Then he opened them and I realised he was slipping in and out of consciousness.

"We got ambushed."

"You," George said to Steve, "over here!"

"What's going on?"

"Move it! And keep your mouth shut," he yelled.

I wondered how long it might be before the shooting and shouting was heard by someone who'd come and investigate or phone the police. But this was waste ground on the other side of train tracks in Hackney where people liked to just mind their own business. So the answer, ages. Steve tried to lift himself, winced at the effort, fell backwards, then manoeuvred himself with one hand, scraping his backside along the ground to get beside me.

"Darren," George called, "move the geezer away from the Merc."

Steve looked over, seeing Ritchie for the first time. He turned to me, his eyes wide, the whites luminous in the gathering dusk.

"What the hell happened?"

"I said shut it!" George roared. Darren grabbed Ritchie's collar and pulled him a yard or two clear of the car, his heels leaving a line in the ground from where he'd come. "Now open the boot," he said to Darren, his eyes and the gun barrel trained on us.

"What you gonna do?" Darren asked.

"Get the suitcases in, do the two over there, then put Terry in the back seat."

"Terry's dead, man!"

"I'm not leaving my brother here. Got it!" George yelled, momentarily turning his back on us. Steve caught my eye.

"What we gonna do?" he mouthed.

I shrugged. There was nothing we could do. There was no way of attacking Norton without getting killed and he wasn't going to be sweet-talked into changing his mind. Sweat began running down my back. I tried to swallow but didn't have the saliva. I'd often wondered how I might die. I hoped it would be at eighty-something in my sleep. It seemed like I was going to be short-changed by forty-odd years.

Darren opened the boot. The cases lay near George. He picked them up, but wouldn't look our way. George moved backwards levelling the rifle at us. Darren dumped the first case in, then the second.

CHAPTER 43

The two bangs, a split second apart, were deep and resonant and full. They completely invaded your hearing, not allowing you to think of anything else. Shutting out anything else. In seconds the Merc's interior was alight with an orange fireball that was so totally overwhelming and complete, it defied tackling. The boot lid and the car doors blew off. Darren disappeared, blown to pieces, jagged fragments of metal spewed somersaulting away in different directions. Steve and I, who fortunately were about twenty feet from the car, were blown backwards. When we'd gathered ourselves we started running and stumbling away as fast as possible. There was another bang, not as loud or as intense, as all the glass exploded, showering us with shards and crystals of Triplex. The fireball inside the Merc spread, its yellow flames licking at the exterior metal.

We managed to reach my motor which had flaked sections of paintwork from the heat, and dents in it from where bits of the Merc had hit it. And then it started snowing! At least that's what I thought until I looked skywards to find a million pounds' worth of banknotes in charred bits and cindered confetti fluttering down on us from the night sky. It settled in our hair, in our mouths, on our clothes, over the Beema. My first thought was 'what a waste'. My second was to be thankful for being so lucky. A few feet closer to the Merc and we'd have been in the same condition as the money.

We sat for a few moments propped against my car. But I knew we'd have to move. Even in 'mind your own business Hackney', it wouldn't be too long before someone reported 'what sounded like a bomb' and the cops would be on their way.

"We gotta go," I said and helped Steve to his feet.

His wound still bled. But not as badly as it had. I opened the car door and helped him stretch out.

"Wait!" he said.

"What?"

"Get my shooter."

"Forget it. It's time to clear off."

"It's got my prints on it."

"Shit! Where did you drop it?"

He pointed to a spot between us and the concrete wall. Where he'd been hit. I crouched low and moved fast shielding my face from the heat. I'd only gone a few yards when I saw George's body half in shadow, half in the orangey glare. He had glass embedded in his face and a long piece of metal impaled in his chest. I moved on, then thought even a piece of rubbish like him was entitled to help if there was a chance, so I went back and felt his neck for a carotid pulse, but there was none.

I made a quick search of his pockets to see if there was anything to connect me with him. His body was damp from all the blood. I found a wallet and tried to remember if I'd ever given him a business card. But I couldn't, so I took it to be on the safe side. Because now wasn't the time to search through it. I found a bunch of keys. I decided to take them to see what there might be of interest in the Merc's boot. Then remembered foolishly, there wasn't a boot because there wasn't a Merc any more. Steve's pump-action was a few feet further on. I grabbed it up, got in the car and took off. George's motor was burning out now. I wondered how long before the cops showed up.

CHAPTER 44

I helped Steve up to his flat over the snooker club by a side entrance. He looked pale and haggard and every so often shivered, though it wasn't cold. I put our shooters under his bed, sat him on the loo seat and looked at his head. He'd been extremely lucky. The bullet had glanced off his temple. It had produced a lot of blood which had matted in his hair, making it thick and stiff. But the wound had stopped bleeding. It was a small jagged hole, the size of a five-pence piece in a flap of flesh with a lot of bruising around it, but not as serious as it looked. Something from way back in my police training, long forgotten, surfaced.

"Well?" he asked.

"The bullet skimmed off, I think it's called the temporalis muscle, something like that. It's the thick muscle that helps you to chew." I filled the sink with warm water and washed the area, cut some hair away, applied iodine and bandaged it.

I helped him to the living room which overlooked the High Road. It was small with alcove cupboards one end and a TV between them. I threw my jacket on an armchair. It fell awkwardly and my fags and keys fell out of the pocket onto the floor. I opened his drinks cabinet beneath some shelving and poured a couple of double Scotches. He downed his in two, held out the glass. But I wouldn't give him another. I sat looking at him thinking how lucky we'd been. Maybe life was just chance ... He sat silent, I supposed reflecting as well.

I wondered about Ritchie's wife and who would tell her what had happened to him. Me or Steve? Poor Ritchie, he'd gone out to earn five hundred quid for a night's work and ended up with a bullet in his chest, propped against a car like a Guy Fawkes with a quizzical look on his untouched face. Like he was trying to work out why he was dead!

"You know, I can still see that fireball inside the car," Steve said. "Shit! That was some bang! All those fucking geezers with their shooters and that show they put on pretending to protect themselves against us when all the time they knew they were going to blow us up. Bastards!" he spat. "What d'you think they used?"

"Semtex in a false bottom, with a remote probably. Because I didn't feel anything when I checked the money. Or maybe in the lid." I should have remembered what Leyton said that night in his flat, that no one seriously puts a million quid in a suitcase.

"If Norton …"

"Don't say it, I know." He shook his head and remembered too late it would hurt. "I'll fetch you some aspirin, then you should get some kip; I'll crash on the sofa in case you need anything in the night. I know a quack who'll fix you up if necessary."

"Thanks Eddie.. I'll burn all our clothes in the morning. You can go home in a tracksuit and a pair of my trainers."

"I'll also need to sort out the car and change the tyres. There's bound to be tracks in the road there."

"Go to Alfie's Tyre Discount, back of Wanstead Junction station. Tell him I sent you and you want the old set seriously lost." He held out his glass.

"No. Too dangerous."

"Listen, if Saxone couldn't kill me or a bomb, a drop more can't." I poured him a nip and told him that was his lot. He took it slower than before but downed it all. "Too bad about the money."

I didn't need reminding. Three weeks' work and all for nothing. Less than nothing because I wouldn't even get my expenses back. I'd expected fifty grand. What I'd got was two beatings and three attempts on my life.

"I can still see Norton's face," he continued, "thinking he'd got the money and then phoof! All confetti and cinders."

I picked up my jacket to get my fags, but the ciggies were on the floor beside my keys. I picked them up and felt keys in my trouser pocket.

"I wonder how long before the cops are on the scene?" Steve asked.

"What?"

"The cops!"

I looked at the keys lying there, George's keys, not mine.

"What about the cops?" I asked.

"What's the matter? Eddie?"

"Nothing." I picked them up and bounced them in my hand.

"Maybe they're there already. What d'you think?" he said.

There were eight or nine on the ring. Yales, deadlocks, a couple of long thin silver ones. I wondered what locks they opened. His house, or maybe a flat. His yard? What if some of the keys were to his yard?

"What?" I replied.

"What's the matter, you got delayed shock or something!"

"No. Just thinking. While you were unconscious George tried to do a deal with Saxone. He said he had nearly a quarter of a mil in readies in his safe at the yard."

"So?"

"Well, the Nortons won't be going back there on account of them being dead."

"Very funny!" He saw the keys in my hand and said, "Oh, no, Eddie! Oh, no!"

"It's unlikely the police can make a positive ID before tomorrow … if then."

"Don't even think about it!"

But I was thinking about it. And the more I thought about it, the more I thought about it. And then something Terry had said downstairs in the snooker club the day he'd tried to bribe me popped into my head. 'We've always got plenty of money on hand. Plenty, and it's always in readies.'

201

"And what if George was just shitting Saxone to buy time?" Steve added. A shrug was the only thing I could offer as a reply. "Three separate attempts to kill you in an hour not enough for you?"

If there was a quarter of a million quid in his safe and I had the keys, then the answer was apparently not.

I took my drink and fag to the window and gave it more thought. The street lights bleached bits of the night, and at 10 p.m. there was still traffic albeit muffled by the double glazing.

"What if these keys are the keys to his yard and safe?"

"What about alarms and maybe a dog?"

"I don't know. It's a breaker's yard, not Fort Knox."

I felt tired, exhausted, shaken by the explosion. And the shock of just how close I'd come to being killed was beginning to catch up on me. But the thought of all that money maybe sitting there just kept going through my mind. What if these were his yard keys? If they were, it was too big a prize to be left to the cops or the Exchequer. By the time I'd finished my drink, I'd decided that if they got me through the gates I'd go for it! If they didn't, because they were keys to do with something else, I'd just get back in the car and come back to Steve's. I told him what I planned to do. He said I was crazy. But it wasn't crazy. Apart from greed it was anger. Anger at having been taken for an idiot for three weeks, at having been beaten up, shot at and blown up with no money to show for it all. Well, maybe a quarter of a million quid would assuage the anger and give me the last laugh!

CHAPTER 45

I drove to my place first to collect a few odds and ends, like a big sports bag, ski mask, bolt cutter, tin of aluminium powder and small brush, a pencil some paper, torches, gloves, and stethoscope. Just the sort of stuff you need for an evening out. Wrens Park Street was a no through road off Brixton Hill. It had trees either side of it, a couple of light industrial units halfway up, and at the top of it, their yard. I turned the car around so that it was facing the way I'd come. Just in case … There were two double iron-mesh gates across the front of the yard secured with a padlock. A large white metal sign attached to them read 'Norton Car Breakers and Parts Specialists' and gleamed in the moonlight.

I put on my mask. The fifth key sprung the padlock. My heart started racing. I could feel the adrenalin surging. My face became flushed from the effort of breathing that found difficulty escaping through the wool of the balaclava. I slipped the chain and slipped inside the yard. I waited for a dog to bark. But none did. The yard was a large oblong area about the size of a small football pitch with a ten-foot wire fence around it. It was badly lit by lights at irregular intervals. It was calm, still, giving it an eerie feeling. A stark comparison with the noise and violence that went on during the day. A light wind swished bits of paper and fag packets making occasional sounds. To one side was a two-storey building. Along the other three sides, rows and rows of cars stacked in twos all with every conceivable damage. Motors without fronts. Without rears. All without wheels, just balanced on top of each other. The only common thing among them a whitewashed stock number painted on the windscreen or on a side if there was no glass. To the left of them was a dump of dozens and dozens of radiators in an open space and beside them a dump of bumpers just left in a heap.

I moved quickly to the building past a crane, its yellow jib high above me; from its claw hung a chain clenched around the roof of a sad little red Micra that just swung in the night as though it had been executed. The building had a CCTV camera mounted above the doorway angled to take in the entrance. I stacked a few tyres behind it, jumped on top of them then clouted the camera with a piece of metal, and the lens popped. Then I forced the camera arm upwards so if it still worked, it recorded nothing but the night and the stars. I crouched underneath the office window. I could feel my heart pounding even harder than before and couldn't understand why people half a mile away couldn't hear it. I eased myself up slowly and peered in. There was a long counter with Dexion shelving behind it running the length of the room, filled with different sizes of boxes, packages and packets. I decided the offices had to be upstairs. I wanted a piss. I wanted a Scotch. But I knew I couldn't have either.

There was a staircase around the side, a metal open-tread affair. The handrails were cold to the touch even through gloves. Twenty feet up it was windy. You could hear the sound of traffic way off on the main road coming to you in a steady staccato hum. The staircase ended in a steel door above which was another CCTV camera. I smashed that lens too and pushed the camera skywards. Beside the door was a numbered security keypad with thick wire running into the wall. I ran my hand over the architrave, turned on my torch and peered at it more closely. The lock was wired to it and to an alarm. Force it or drill it and it would go off.

The thing about having been a copper, it helps you think like a villain. Always useful when you're up to a bit of villainy yourself. That's why I'd brought the aluminium powder with me. It's what cops use to dust for fingerprints. But it has other uses as well. I applied it with a small brush over the keys of the pad then waited a few moments. Then shone a small ultraviolet torch over them. People spend thousands on security. But forget about common sense. There were ten buttons. One to nine and zero. Under the ultraviolet light seven buttons were clean and gleamed because they were never touched. Numbers one, five and nine were scuffed and grimy because they were the ones continually pressed. I wrote down the only six combinations you can make of three numbers and started pressing. The door clicked open on the fourth attempt, nine, five, one. I stepped inside. It was as easy as that. Not really a problem, if you think like a villain!

There was no hallway or entrance. You just stepped off the stairs into the office. I switched on my regular torch. A small circle of light played around the room. There were two desks facing each other with chairs behind them. One desk had a pair of phones on it and an answerphone, twinkling in the dark. The other had plastic teacups and burger boxes across it. There were a couple of filing cabinets in the corner and on a small table beside them, the CD video recorder for the CCTV. I pressed stop, release, and pocketed the CD.

The safe was at the back. I pulled a small computer table out of the way and got in front of it and shone my torch and became silhouetted on the wall behind it. The suddenness of it appearing in front of me so starkly almost made me jump. The safe was a pre-war Milner, hardened steel about four feet high, two feet wide and who knew how thick. The front just had keyholes top and bottom of it and a handle. I swapped the rubber gloves for thin white latex ones. I ran my hands around the safe. There were no wires or cables to or from it. Then I put the bell of a stethoscope over it but could detect no pulses or hum. It seemed to me it was just a key and handle job.

I looked at George's keys. The likely candidates were the long slim silver ones. If they worked I was in. If they didn't I was on my way back to Steve's, because I'm okay as far as a bit of breaking and entering is concerned. But a safe cracker, or locksmith, I'm not. I slid one of the keys into the top keyhole but it wouldn't turn. So I stuck it in the bottom one and it did. I stuck the second key in the top hole and that turned. I pulled the handle down and abra-fucking-cadabra!

I pulled the door wide open and shone my torch inside. There was a shelf with a cardboard box on it. Below it a bigger cardboard box filled with banknotes. Fifties. I guessed about a hundred to a bundle secured with elastic bands. Perhaps forty or fifty bundles all nicely waiting to be stolen. I stood there for a moment or two just looking at it all. Not really believing what I saw. All I could do was smile. I just stood there like an idiot grinning. And then I came to my senses, opened the sports bag and dumped the money in it. I opened the smaller box, log books, MOT certificates, ledgers, and a small notebook with columns across double pages headed name, telephone number, car make, reg, price. Each column had items under it. I couldn't make sense of it. But on impulse threw it into the bag, with my torches, powder, brush — everything. Then looked about to make sure I'd not left anything. I closed and re-locked the safe, checked again I'd not dropped anything, then put the computer table back in place because it was time-to-go time. I closed the office door, then the yard gates and re-padlocked them, dumped the bag in the boot with my ski mask and gloves and headed for Steve's. All things being equal no one would ever know I'd been there! It's as easy as that, if you think like a villain!

CHAPTER 46

I rang the doorbell a few times, then heard him on the stairs. He opened up bleary-eyed and I guessed I'd woken him. He looked at me and said,

"I don't need to ask. I can tell from your face."

I followed him up to the living room. There was an unfinished ham sandwich on the coffee table beside an unfinished Scotch.

"How's your head?"

"Sore. But I'll live. Well?"

"Sweet as a nut!"

"How much?"

"I didn't count it. But I reckon a couple hundred grand!"

"Nice one!" And this time it was his turn to smile. "Any problems?"

I told him about the CCTV cameras. But apart from that, it had been a doddle.

"I'll throw the keys away tomorrow. One by one, in a dustbin, down a drain, in a builder's skip, usual MO."

I had some coffee and a sandwich. Then began counting the money, which I'd turfed out onto the carpet. There were a lot of notes. Crisp ones, creased ones, clean ones, dirty ones. But mainly all in my favourite colour, Bank of England red. It took ninety minutes. It came to two hundred and fifty thousand, six hundred and fifty quid. I divided it into four lots. Thirty grand for Steve who at first refused to take it then relented. Twenty grand for Ritchie's wife, and a hundred grand each for me and Lisa. The odd six hundred and fifty I kept for petrol money, well ...!

It was two in the morning, but I was high on the sight of all that wonga …

"What d'you make of this?" I asked Steve tossing him George's notebook. "It was in the safe along with the dosh."

He looked it over and yawned. Turned a few pages and yawned again.

"Interesting. Looks like a record of bent car deals. They sell two halves of separate cars either dumped or insurance write-offs to these people," he said tapping the page. "They weld the two good bits together and sell them on as kosher."

"Bastards! That's presumably where all this dough comes from."

"You should send this to the Met's Car Crime Squad," he said throwing it back. "They'll have a field day with all these names and telephone numbers!"

"No, I'll send it to Stafford anonymously. He can turn it over to them. That way they'll owe him. He'll like that. I'll include the photocopy of the drafts. It'll be like a guided missile working its way right back to Belgium. It'll serve those bastards right for trying to kill us. It can't hurt the gang because they're all dead. So no comeback this end, apart from Ralph and his Hatton Garden mate. What d'you think?" But there was no reply. Steve had fallen asleep, his bandaged head propped by the cushions. His feet dangling over the end of the sofa. I dropped the notebook on the coffee table and drifted off myself. And why not? One way and another, it had been quite a night!

CHAPTER 47

I phoned Lisa the next morning. She asked what had happened about George and Terry. I told her it was sorted and that she could go back home. Then I told her I had some money for her.

"That was quick."

"A hundred grand!"

"Jesus! That's just fantastic, Eddie. That's absolutely brilliant. You've no idea what this money will mean." Then her voice dropped a bit. "It's fifty–fifty like we agreed. Right? Fifty grand a-piece?"

"No."

"What?"

"It's a hundred each. In cash."

"But how?"

"You don't want to know! You just need somewhere safe to keep it. Because you can't bank it. And you can't put it in a building society, comprende?"

"Oh, Eddie! Eddie! Thank you, I can't believe it! A hundred grand!" she squealed. "Thank you!"

"Don't mention it."

"You know I still owe you that drink I promised."

"So you do!" I recalled the pair of us in the hotel corridor. Her getting more and more excited, pressing herself closer and closer to me as she watched me undo the door number. "So you do," I repeated. We made a date for that evening and I found myself looking forward to seeing her.

THE END

www.ingramcontent.com/pod-product-compliance
Lightning Source LLC
Chambersburg PA
CBHW020951180626
46814CB00003B/1032